THE MERCHANT OF VENICE

（中英文双语对照）

孙大雨　译

【英】威廉·莎士比亚　著

威尼斯商人

上海三联书店

THE MERCHANT of VENICE

DRAMATIS PERSONAE

The Duke of Venice

The Prince of Morocco, suitor to Portia

The Prince of Arragon, suitor to Portia

Antonio, a merchant of Venice

Bassanio, his friend, suitor likewise to Portia

Salanio, friend to Antonio and Bassanio

Salarino, friend to Antonio and Bassanio

Gratiano, friend to Antonio and Bassanio

Lorenzo, in love with Jessica

Shylock, a rich Jew

Tubal, a Jew, his friend

Launcelot Gobbo, a clown, servant to Shylock

Old Gobbo, father to Launcelot

Leonardo, servant to Bassanio

Balthasar, servant to Portia

Stephano, servant to Portia

Portia, a rich heiress

Nerissa, her waiting-maid

Jessica, daughter to Shylock

剧 中 人 物

威尼斯公爵

摩洛哥亲王
阿拉贡亲王 } 宝喜霞的求婚者

安东尼奥,威尼斯商人

跋萨尼奥,安东尼奥的朋友,也是宝喜霞的求婚者

萨拉尼奥
萨拉里诺 } 安东尼奥与跋萨尼奥的朋友
葛拉希阿诺

洛良佐,絜雪格的恋人

夏洛克,犹太富翁

屠勃尔,犹太人,夏洛克的朋友

朗斯洛忒·高卜,小丑,夏洛克的仆人

老高卜,朗斯洛忒的父亲

里奥哪铎,跋萨尼奥的仆人

鲍尔萨什
斯丹法诺 } 宝喜霞的仆人

宝喜霞,富家嗣女

纳丽莎,宝喜霞的陪娘

絜雪格,夏洛克的女儿

Magnificoes of Venice, Officers of the Court of Justice, Gaoler, Servants to Portia, and other Attendants

SCENE: Partly at Venice; and partly at Belmont; the seat of Portia; on the Continent

威尼斯众显贵、法院官吏、狱卒、宝喜霞的仆从及其他随从

剧景：一部分在威尼斯；一部分在大陆上的贝尔蒙；宝喜霞的邸宅所在地

ACT I.

SCENE I. Venice. *A street*

[*Enter* Antonio, Salarino, *and* Salanio]

Antonio   In sooth, I know not why I am so sad;
It wearies me; you say it wearies you;
But how I caught it, found it, or came by it,
What stuff 'tis made of, whereof it is born,
I am to learn;
And such a want-wit sadness makes of me
That I have much ado to know myself.

Salarino   Your mind is tossing on the ocean;
There where your argosies, with portly sail—
Like signiors and rich burghers on the flood,
Or as it were the pageants of the sea—
Do overpeer the petty traffickers,
That curtsy to them, do them reverence,
As they fly by them with their woven wings.

Salanio   Believe me, sir, had I such venture forth,
The better part of my affections would
Be with my hopes abroad. I should be still
Plucking the grass to know where sits the wind,

第 一 幕

第 一 景

[威尼斯。一街道]

[安东尼奥、萨拉里诺与萨拉尼奥上。

安 东 尼 奥 当真,我不懂为什么我这样忧郁:
我为此厌烦;你们说,也觉得厌烦;
我可怎么会沾上它,怎么会碰到它,
这忧郁是因何而形成,怎么会产生,
我却不知道;
忧郁将我变成了这样个呆子,
简直叫我自己也莫名其妙。

萨 拉 里 诺 您的心当是在大海洋上翻腾;
那儿,您那些张着巨帆的海舶,
如同洪波大浪上的显要和豪商,
或者像海上的华彩物景展览台,
高高俯瞰着一些轻捷的小商舸,
当它们张开编织的翅膀飞过时,
众小艇对它们弯腰屈膝齐致敬。

萨 拉 尼 奥 相信我,仁君,若有这买卖风险
在外洋,我定必要用多半的心思
牵挂着它。我也兀自会总要
去摘取草标,探测风吹的方向,

Peering in maps for ports, and piers, and roads;
And every object that might make me fear
Misfortune to my ventures, out of doubt
Would make me sad.

Salarino   My wind, cooling my broth
Would blow me to an ague, when I thought
What harm a wind too great might do at sea.
I should not see the sandy hour-glass run
But I should think of shallows and of flats,
And see my wealthy Andrew dock'd in sand,
Vailing her high top lower than her ribs
To kiss her burial. Should I go to church
And see the holy edifice of stone,
And not bethink me straight of dangerous rocks,
Which, touching but my gentle vessel's side,
Would scatter all her spices on the stream,
Enrobe the roaring waters with my silks,
And, in a word, but even now worth this,
And now worth nothing? Shall I have the thought
To think on this, and shall I lack the thought
That such a thing bechanc'd would make me sad?
But tell not me; I know Antonio
Is sad to think upon his merchandise.

Antonio   Believe me, no; I thank my fortune for it,
My ventures are not in one bottom trusted,
Nor to one place; nor is my whole estate
Upon the fortune of this present year;
Therefore my merchandise makes me not sad.

Salarino   Why, then you are in love.

Antonio   Fie, fie!

Salarino   Not in love neither? Then let us say you are sad
Because you are not merry; and 'twere as easy
For you to laugh and leap and say you are merry,

找寻地图上的港口、埠头、碇泊所；
凡是能叫我担心我所冒风险
会遭到灾难的每件事情，这疑虑
都使我忧郁。

萨拉里诺　　　　　　　我吹凉肉汤的呼气
会引起我一阵寒颤，当我想到了
海上太大的一阵风会肇多大祸。
当我一见到计时的沙漏在漏沙，
我马上想到的乃是浅滩和沙洲，
把它的桅尖埋得比龙肋还要低，
去吻它的葬地。我若去到礼拜堂，
望见那神圣而巍峨的石砌大厦，
哪有不马上想到磊磊的礁石
只一碰我那轻盈的大船船舷，
就会把一舱的香料都倒在浪里，
使咆哮的海涛穿上我的丝绸匹头，
而且，一句话，这会儿值得如许多，
那会儿不值一个钱？我怎能想起
这么一件事，而竟然不去想到
假如这样的事发生，我一定得忧郁？
不用跟我说；我知道，安东尼奥
乃是为担心他的货运而发愁。

安东尼奥　相信我，不是的；我要感谢我的命运，
我所担的风险不寄托在一艘船上，
也不靠一处地方，我全部的经营
也不托赖着目今这一年的运会。
所以我装船的货品不使我忧郁。

萨拉里诺　对了，那您是在恋爱。

安东尼奥　　　　　　　　呸，开玩笑！

萨拉里诺　也不在恋爱？那么，我们说您忧郁，
因为您不是在欢乐：那就很容易，
当见您又笑又跳时，就说您欢乐，

Because you are not sad. Now, by two-headed Janus,
Nature hath fram'd strange fellows in her time:
Some that will evermore peep through their eyes,
And laugh like parrots at a bag-piper;
And other of such vinegar aspect
That they'll not show their teeth in way of smile
Though Nestor swear the jest be laughable.

[*Enter* Bassanio, Lorenzo, *and* Gratiano.]

Salanio   Here comes Bassanio, your most noble kinsman,
Gratiano, and Lorenzo. Fare ye well;
We leave you now with better company.

Salarino   I would have stay'd till I had made you merry,
If worthier friends had not prevented me.

Antonio   Your worth is very dear in my regard.
I take it your own business calls on you,
And you embrace th' occasion to depart.

Salarino   Good morrow, my good lords.

Bassanio   Good signiors both, when shall we laugh? Say
when.
You grow exceeding strange; must it be so?

Salarino   We'll make our leisures to attend on yours.

[*Exeunt* Salarino *and* Salanio.]

Lorenzo   My Lord Bassanio, since you have found An-
tonio,
We two will leave you; but at dinner-time,
I pray you, have in mind where we must meet.

Bassanio   I will not fail you.

Gratiano   You look not well, Signior Antonio;
You have too much respect upon the world;
They lose it that do buy it with much care.
Believe me, you are marvellously chang'd.

Antonio   I hold the world but as the world, Gratiano;
A stage, where every man must play a part,
And mine a sad one.

Gratiano   Let me play the fool;
With mirth and laughter let old wrinkles come;

因为您不忧郁。我凭两面神耶纳斯
起个誓，天公创造人造得好奇怪：
有些人永远眯着眼偷窥而笑，
像鹦鹉瞧见吹风笛的人一般；
有些个却总是满脸的酸醋味儿，
从不会露出牙齿笑那么一下，
即使奈斯托打赌那笑话很好笑。

〔跋萨尼奥、洛良佐与葛拉希阿诺上。

萨 拉 尼 奥	您的最尊贵的亲戚跋萨尼奥，
	葛拉希阿诺和洛良佐来了。再见：
	我们告别了，让位给更好的友伴。
萨 拉 里 诺	若不是您两位高贵的朋友来了，
	我准会待下来，直到逗得您欢笑。
安 东 尼 奥	二位高华的品德我十分尊视。
	我意想你们自己有事情要干，
	故而借这个机会辞别了离开。
萨 拉 里 诺	祝各位早安。
跋 萨 尼 奥	两位仁兄，何时能相叙共谈笑？
	你们显得生疏了：一定得如此吗？
萨 拉 里 诺	您何时有空，我们随时好奉陪。

〔萨拉里诺与萨拉尼奥下。

洛 良 佐	跋萨尼奥公子，您见了安东尼奥，
	我们两人就告别：但午饭时分，
	请您要记得我们在哪里相会。
跋 萨 尼 奥	我准时不失约。
葛拉希阿诺	您神色不太好，安东尼奥大兄长；
	您把世事看待得太过认真了：
	太花了心思作代价，反倒会失着：
	请信我这话，您远非前一晌可比。
安 东 尼 奥	我把这世界当世界，葛拉希阿诺；
	当作每人要演个角色的舞台，
	我演的是个悲苦角。
葛拉希阿诺	我来演丑角。
	让皱纹跟欢乐和哗笑一起来到，

And let my liver rather heat with wine
Than my heart cool with mortifying groans.
Why should a man whose blood is warm within
Sit like his grandsire cut in alabaster,
Sleep when he wakes, and creep into the jaundice
By being peevish? I tell thee what, Antonio—
I love thee, and 'tis my love that speaks—
There are a sort of men whose visages
Do cream and mantle like a standing pond,
And do a wilful stillness entertain,
With purpose to be dress'd in an opinion
Of wisdom, gravity, profound conceit;
As who should say *I am Sir Oracle*,
And when I ope my lips let no dog bark.
O my Antonio, I do know of these
That therefore only are reputed wise
For saying nothing; when, I am very sure,
If they should speak, would almost damn those ears
Which, hearing them, would call their brothers fools.
I'll tell thee more of this another time.
But fish not with this melancholy bait,
For this fool gudgeon, this opinion.
Come, good Lorenzo. Fare ye well awhile;
I'll end my exhortation after dinner.

Lorenzo Well, we will leave you then till dinner-time.
I must be one of these same dumb wise men,
For Gratiano never lets me speak.

Gratiano Well, keep me company but two years moe,
Thou shalt not know the sound of thine own tongue.

Antonio Fare you well; I'll grow a talker for this gear.

Gratiano Thanks, i' faith, for silence is only commendable
In a neat's tongue dried, and a maid not vendible.

　　　　　　而且宁愿我的肝用酒来温热，
　　　　　　别叫我的心给痛苦的悲吟吹冷。
　　　　　　为什么一个人，他的血液是暖的，
　　　　　　要像他祖父的雪花石膏像，骏坐着？
　　　　　　醒来时还在睡，无端地乖张生气，
　　　　　　害一场黄疸病？告诉您，安东尼奥——
　　　　　　我对您友爱，爱上您所以这么说——
　　　　　　这世上有一类人儿，他们的脸色，
　　　　　　像死水池塘，萍藻掩盖着天光，
　　　　　　操持一片执意要沉默的冷气，
　　　　　　目的无非是要人家认为他为人
　　　　　　多智慧，神态端庄，和思想深宏，
　　　　　　他仿佛在说，"我是在宣读神谕；
　　　　　　我开口说话时，不许有狗儿嗥叫！"
　　　　　　老兄啊，安东尼奥，我知道这些人
　　　　　　只是因此上有了智慧的名声，
　　　　　　由于不开腔，可是我却很明白，
　　　　　　假使他们要说话，会叫人两耳
　　　　　　受罪罚，听到的就会骂他们傻瓜。
　　　　　　我下回再跟您来谈这件事儿：
　　　　　　可是别用愁闷这钓饵来垂钓了，
　　　　　　去钓取那无聊得很的虚名俗誉。
　　　　　　来吧，洛良佐老兄。小别一下子：
　　　　　　午饭过后，我再来结束这劝告。

洛　良　佐　好吧，我们跟你们小别到吃饭时：
　　　　　　我准是一个他说的紧口聪明人，
　　　　　　因为葛拉希阿诺从不让我讲。

葛拉希阿诺　得，跟我在一起再过上两年啊，
　　　　　　管保你认不出你自个儿的口音。

安　东　尼　奥　祝安好：我要学会多讲点话儿咧。

葛拉希阿诺　多谢，当真，为的是沉默只适于
　　　　　　干的牛门腔、嫁不掉的老处女。

[*Exeunt* Gratiano *and* Lorenzo.]

Antonio   Is that anything now?

Bassanio   Gratiano speaks an infinite deal of nothing, more than any man in all Venice. His reasons are as two grains of wheat hid in, two bushels of chaff: you shall seek all day ere you find them, and when you have them they are not worth the search.

Antonio   Well; tell me now what lady is the same
To whom you swore a secret pilgrimage,
That you to-day promis'd to tell me of?

Bassanio   'Tis not unknown to you, Antonio,
How much I have disabled mine estate
By something showing a more swelling port
Than my faint means would grant continuance;
Nor do I now make moan to be abridg'd
From such a noble rate; but my chief care
Is to come fairly off from the great debts
Wherein my time, something too prodigal,
Hath left me gag'd. To you, Antonio,
I owe the most, in money and in love;
And from your love I have a warranty
To unburden all my plots and purposes
How to get clear of all the debts I owe.

Antonio   I pray you, good Bassanio, let me know it;
And if it stand, as you yourself still do,
Within the eye of honour, be assur'd
My purse, my person, my extremest means,
Lie all unlock'd to your occasions.

Bassanio   In my school-days, when I had lost one shaft,
I shot his fellow of the self-same flight
The self-same way, with more advised watch,
To find the other forth; and by adventuring both
I oft found both. I urge this childhood proof,

〔葛拉希阿诺与洛良佐下。

安东尼奥　这一车话儿可有些什么?

跋萨尼奥　葛拉希阿诺比整个威尼斯城里不论谁都更扯得一大
　　　　　车废话。他的理数好像是两箩筐秕糠里藏着的两颗
　　　　　麦粒:你找了一整天才找到它们,找到后你觉得不值
　　　　　得找。

安东尼奥　好吧,告诉我谁是那一位闺秀?
　　　　　你立誓要去向她作秘密的参拜,
　　　　　你曾答允今天会要告诉我。

跋萨尼奥　安东尼奥,你不是未有所闻知,
　　　　　只因我为了维持虚有的外表,
　　　　　而我的资源太微薄,不胜挥霍,
　　　　　我已经多么伤残了我的财货:
　　　　　如今我倒也并不为境况清寒
　　　　　而叹息伤感;但是我主要的烦恼
　　　　　乃是在设法解除我肩头的重债,
　　　　　由于我过去浪费太多而深深
　　　　　陷入了这困境。对于你,安东尼奥,
　　　　　我亏欠太大,友爱和金钱同样多,
　　　　　而为了你爱我,我就作为是许可,
　　　　　把我怎样定下了计划和目的,
　　　　　去清除债务,全部来向你诉说。

安东尼奥　好跋萨尼奥,要请你让我晓得;
　　　　　倘使能符合光荣和正道,如同
　　　　　你现在仍然是这样,你尽可安心,
　　　　　我的钱囊和身家,竭尽我的一切,
　　　　　都毫无保留地供你驱遣使用。

跋萨尼奥　在我的求学年间,射失了一支箭,
　　　　　我便发射另一支同样的羽镞,
　　　　　向着同一个方向,注视得较真切,
　　　　　去寻找先前的那支,冒险了两支,
　　　　　我终于都找到;我举这童年事例,

Because what follows is pure innocence.
I owe you much; and, like a wilful youth,
That which I owe is lost; but if you please
To shoot another arrow that self way
Which you did shoot the first, I do not doubt,
As I will watch the aim, or to find both,
Or bring your latter hazard back again
And thankfully rest debtor for the first.

Antonio   You know me well, and herein spend but time
To wind about my love with circumstance;
And out of doubt you do me now more wrong
In making question of my uttermost
Than if you had made waste of all I have.
Then do but say to me what I should do
That in your knowledge may by me be done,
And I am prest unto it; therefore, speak.

Bassanio   In Belmont is a lady richly left,
And she is fair and, fairer than that word,
Of wondrous virtues. Sometimes from her eyes
I did receive fair speechless messages:
Her name is Portia—nothing undervalu'd
To Cato's daughter, Brutus' Portia:
Nor is the wide world ignorant of her worth,
For the four winds blow in from every coast
Renowned suitors, and her sunny locks
Hang on her temples like a golden fleece;
Which makes her seat of Belmont Colchos' strond,
And many Jasons come in quest of her.
O my Antonio! had I but the means
To hold a rival place with one of them,
I have a mind presages me such thrift
That I should questionless be fortunate.

只因我接着说的也天真而幼稚。
我对你负欠太多，但年轻而任性，
欠你的我已经失掉；可是假如你
乐意向同一方向再发一支箭，
去追踪那初次的发射，我敢确信，
我看得真切，两支箭会一同找到，
或至少要把你两次的冒险收回，
而感念你初次的恩情，再图奉璧。

安东尼奥 你熟知我的情意，如今只空费
时间，迂回曲折地试探我的爱；
你心存疑虑，不信我会竭尽了
全力来解脱你的困厄，这就比
耗尽我全部的所有，还更加见外：
故而，只要告诉我，我该怎么办，
你认为我可以对你有所帮助，
那就一准来做到：所以，你说啊。

跋萨尼奥 贝尔蒙城里有一位丰殷的孤女，
她姿容绝妙，而尤其卓越难得的
是她那芳华的美德：我从她眼里
曾受到秋水流波的含情顾盼：
她名叫宝喜霞，比古时坎托之女，
勃鲁德的贤妻宝喜霞寥无逊色：
这广大的世界耳闻她的贤良美妙，
但见四方的好风从各处海滨
吹来了声名籍籍的求婚佳客。
从她两鬓垂下来的华发则宛如
神话里的金羊毛，使她的贝尔蒙成了
科尔契王邦，有许多鉴逊来探访。
啊，我的好安东尼奥，只要我
囊橐充盈，能够跟他们相匹敌，
我心头有预见，指望得好运来临，
准能完成我那如花的美梦。

Antonio   Thou know'st that all my fortunes are at sea;
Neither have I money nor commodity
To raise a present sum; therefore go forth,
Try what my credit can in Venice do;
That shall be rack'd, even to the uttermost,
To furnish thee to Belmont to fair Portia.
Go presently inquire, and so will I,
Where money is; and I no question make
To have it of my trust or for my sake.

[Exeunt.]

SCENE II. Belmont. *A room in Portia's house*

[Enter Portia and Nerissa.]

Portia   By my troth, Nerissa, my little body is aweary of
this great world.

Nerissa   You would be, sweet madam, if your miseries
were in the same abundance as your good fortunes
are; and yet, for aught I see, they are as sick that
surfeit with too much as they that starve with nothing. It is no mean happiness, therefore, to be seated
in the mean: superfluity come sooner by white hairs,
but competency lives longer.

Portia   Good sentences, and well pronounced.

Nerissa   They would be better, if well followed.

Portia   If to do were as easy as to know what were good
to do, chapels had been churches, and poor men's
cottages princes' palaces. It is a good divine that follows his own instructions; I can easier teach twenty
what were good to be done than to be one of the twenty to follow mine own teaching. The brain may devise
laws for the blood, but a hot temper leaps o'er a cold
decree; such a hare is madness the youth, to skip o'er
the meshes of good counsel the cripple. But this rea-
soning is not in the fashion to choose me a husband.

安 东 尼 奥　　你知道我全部资产都在海上；
　　　　　　　我既无现金，又没有货赇去筹措
　　　　　　　一大笔款项：故而且到市上去；
　　　　　　　试我的信用能在威尼斯怎么样：
　　　　　　　要竭尽我的信用的能耐去筹款，
　　　　　　　供应你能到贝尔蒙，去找宝喜霞。
　　　　　　　去吧，马上去探问，我自己也就去，
　　　　　　　哪里有款子，我不问条件好歹，
　　　　　　　不论作为我担保，或作为我借贷。

　　　　　　　　　　　　　　　　　　　〔同下

第 二 景

〔贝尔蒙。宝喜霞邸内一室〕
〔宝喜霞与纳丽莎上。

宝　喜　霞　　当真，纳丽莎，我这小小的身体实在经受不了这个大
　　　　　　　世界。
纳　丽　莎　　您是会受不了的，好姑娘，如果您的苦恼跟您那好运
　　　　　　　道一般多：可是，由我看来，那些吃得太饱的人跟那
　　　　　　　些挨饿没东西吃的同样要病倒。所以，居于中庸地
　　　　　　　带并不能算作不快乐：富裕会催生白发，但适中能引
　　　　　　　出长寿。
宝　喜　霞　　好话，讲得对。
纳　丽　莎　　要是能照着做，那就更好了。
宝　喜　霞　　倘使实地去做一件事跟知道什么好事可以做同样容
　　　　　　　易，小教堂会变成大寺院，穷人的草屋会变成王侯的
　　　　　　　宫殿了。一位好的传教师才会遵从他自己的教诲：
　　　　　　　我更容易教二十个人做什么好事，却不能做二十个
　　　　　　　人中间的一个，去按我自己的教训行事。理智可以
　　　　　　　帮助制定法律约束感情，但激情会跳过冷静的律令：
　　　　　　　青年的狂热是这样一只野兔，它会跳过忠告这跛子
　　　　　　　的法网。可是这样说理不能替我挑选一个丈夫。唉

O me, the word choose! I may neither choose who I would nor refuse who I dislike; so is the will of a living daughter curb'd by the will of a dead father. Is it not hard, Nerissa, that I cannot choose one, nor refuse none?

Nerissa Your father was ever virtuous, and holy men at their death have good inspirations; therefore the lott'ry that he hath devised in these three chests, of gold, silver, and lead, whereof who chooses his meaning chooses you, will no doubt never be chosen by any rightly but one who you shall rightly love. But what warmth is there in your affection towards any of these princely suitors that are already come?

Portia I pray thee over-name them; and as thou namest them, I will describe them; and according to my description, level at my affection.

Nerissa First, there is the Neapolitan prince.

Portia Ay, that's a colt indeed, for he doth nothing but talk of his horse; and he makes it a great appropriation to his own good parts that he can shoe him himself; I am much afeard my lady his mother play'd false with a smith.

Nerissa Then is there the County Palatine.

Portia He doth nothing but frown, as who should say *An you will not have me*, *choose*. He hears merry tales and smiles not: I fear he will prove the weeping philosopher when he grows old, being so full of unmannerly sadness in his youth. I had rather be married to a death's-head with a bone in his mouth than to either of these. God defend me from these two!

Nerissa How say you by the French lord, Monsieur Le Bon?

Portia God made him, and therefore let him pass for a man. In truth, I know it is a sin to be a mocker, but he! why, he hath a horse better than the Neapolitan's, a better bad habit of frowning than the Count Palatine; he is every man in no man. If a throstle sing he falls straight a-capering; he will fence with his own shadow; if I should marry him, I should marry twenty husbands. If he would despise me, I would forgive him; for if he love me to madness, I shall never requite him.

哟,说到挑选!我既不能挑选我所喜爱的,也不能拒绝我所厌恶的;一个活着的女儿的意志便这样被一个死了的父亲的遗嘱所控制。纳丽莎,我不能拒绝,也不能挑选,岂不是难受吗?

纳　丽　莎　您父亲素来是有德的;道德高尚的人临终时必有颖悟:故而拈阄,在他设计的金、银、铅三只匣子里挑选一只,谁挑对了他的用意就挑中了您,无疑,除非他是真正爱您,否则决不会被拈对。可是您对这几位已经来到的公侯贵胄中哪一位求婚人,比较有好感?

宝　喜　霞　你且把他们一个个道来;你提名以后,我来描摹他们几句,从我的道白里,你可以觉察到我的感情。

纳　丽　莎　首先,那位那坡利亲王。

宝　喜　霞　嗨,那真是匹小马,因为他不讲别的,只谈他的马儿;因为他当作他的大好本领,能自己钉马蹄铁。我只恐他的令堂大人跟一个铁匠有过花头。

纳　丽　莎　然后是那位巴拉廷伯爵。

宝　喜　霞　他一天到晚颦眉蹙额,仿佛说"假如你不爱我,算了":他听到好笑的故事也不笑:我只恐他到了老年会变成个哭泣哲人,如今这么年轻已经愁眉苦脸得不像样子。我宁愿嫁给一个骷髅,它嘴里插一根骨头,也不愿嫁这两个里边的哪一个。上帝保佑我别让他们拈中了我!

纳　丽　莎　那位法兰西贵族勒·榜先生,您对他怎么说?

宝　喜　霞　上帝造下了他,故而就算他是个人。说实在话,我知道嘲笑人是一桩罪辜:可是他呀!唉,他有一匹比那坡利人更好的马,比那巴拉廷伯爵更糟的皱眉恶习;他是各式各样的人混和在一起,可没有他自己,听到一只画眉在鸣,他马上会跳跃:他会同他自己的影子斗剑:我若是嫁了他,就嫁了二十个丈夫。他如果瞧不上我,我会原谅他,因为他如果爱得我发了疯,我决不会报答他的恩情。

Nerissa What say you, then, to Falconbridge, the young baron of England?

Portia You know I say nothing to him, for he understands not me, nor I him; he hath neither Latin, French, nor I-talian, and you will come into the court and swear that I have a poor pennyworth in the English. He is a proper man's picture; but alas, who can converse with a dumb-show? How oddly he is suited! I think he bought his doublet in Italy, his round hose in France, his bonnet in Germany, and his behaviour everywhere.

Nerissa What think you of the Scottish lord, his neigh-bour?

Portia That he hath a neighbourly charity in him, for he borrowed a box of the ear of the Englishman, and swore he would pay him again when he was able; I think the Frenchman became his surety, and sealed under for another.

Nerissa How like you the young German, the Duke of Saxony's nephew?

Portia Very vilely in the morning when he is sober, and most vilely in the afternoon when he is drunk; when he is best, he is a little worse than a man, and when he is worst, he is little better than a beast. An the worst fall that ever fell, I hope I shall make shift to go without him.

Nerissa If he should offer to choose, and choose the right casket, you should refuse to perform your father's will, if you should refuse to accept him.

Portia Therefore, for fear of the worst, I pray thee set a deep glass of Rhenish wine on the contrary casket; for if the devil be within and that temptation without, I know he will choose it. I will do anything, Nerissa, ere I will be married to a sponge.

Nerissa You need not fear, lady, the having any of these lords; they have acquainted me with their determina-tions, which is indeed to return to their home, and to trouble you with no more suit, unless you may be won by some other sort than your father's imposition, de-pending on the caskets.

Portia If I live to be as old as Sibylla, I will die as chaste as Diana, unless I be obtained by the manner of my father's will. I am glad this parcel of wooers are so reasonable; for there is not one among them but I dote on his very absence, and I pray God grant them a fair departure.

纳 丽 莎　那么,您对那位英格兰青年男爵福康勃立琪怎么说?

宝 喜 霞　你知道我不跟他说话,因为他不懂我的话,我也不懂他的话:他不会说拉丁、法兰西话,也不说意大利话,而你可以到法庭上去宣誓,我的英格兰话不值一个钱。他的外表还可以,可是,啊,谁能跟一个打手势的哑巴开谈?他的穿戴多古怪!我想他的短裤是在意大利买的,紧身裤是在法国买的,软帽是在德国买的,而他的举止是从天南地北弄来的。

纳 丽 莎　您认为他的邻居,那位苏格兰贵族怎样?

宝 喜 霞　他对邻居讲信修睦,因为他曾出借给那英格兰人一记耳光,他便发誓要在他能办到的时候偿还那记耳光:我想那法兰西人为他作保,立证签约,定必清偿。

纳 丽 莎　您看那青年德意志人,萨克逊公爵的侄子,怎样?

宝 喜 霞　早上他清醒时已经很坏,下午他喝醉了实在太糟:他最好时比一个人稍微坏些,最坏时比畜生略好一些:倘使最不幸的事发生,我希望我能设法不跟他在一起。

纳 丽 莎　要是他要求挑选,选中了那只中彩的匣子,您会拒绝遵循您父亲的遗嘱,如果您拒绝接他为夫婿的话。

宝 喜 霞　故而,为避免遭殃,你务必在一只差错的匣儿上放上深深一杯莱茵河葡萄酒,因为倘然魔鬼在里边作怪而诱惑在外面,我知道他会要去挑选。我什么事都可以去做,纳丽莎,可不能嫁给一个醉鬼。

纳 丽 莎　姑娘,您不用害怕会配上这些贵胄们的任何一位:他们已经告诉我他们的决心;那就是的确要回家去,不再麻烦您向您求婚,除非求得您能用别的办法,不照您父亲规定的经过挑选匣儿去解决。

宝 喜 霞　假使活到古代神巫那样老,我要跟月亮女神黛安娜一样贞洁,除非能按照先父的遗嘱办理娶得我。我高兴这一帮求婚人这么懂事,因为他们之中没有一个我不切望他离开的;祈求上帝赐他们以好风。

Nerissa   Do you not remember, lady, in your father's time, a Venetian, a scholar and a soldier, that came hither in company of the Marquis of Montferrat?

Portia   Yes, yes, it was Bassanio; as I think, so was he called.

Nerissa   True, madam; he, of all the men that ever my foolish eyes looked upon, was the best deserving a fair lady.

Portia   I remember him well, and I remember him worthy of thy praise.

[*Enter a* Servant.]

How now! what news?

Servant   The four strangers seek for you, madam, to take their leave; and there is a forerunner come from a fifth, the Prince of Morocco, who brings word the Prince his master will be here to-night.

Portia   If I could bid the fifth welcome with so good heart as I can bid the other four farewell, I should be glad of his approach; if he have the condition of a saint and the complexion of a devil, I had rather he should shrive me than wive me.

Come, Nerissa. Sirrah, go before.

Whiles we shut the gate upon one wooer, another knocks at the door.   [*Exeunt.*]

SCENE III. Venice. *A public place*

[*Enter* Bassanio *and* Shylock.]

Shylock   *Three thousand ducats*; well?

Bassanio   Ay, sir, for three months.

Shylock   *For three months*; well?

Bassanio   For the which, as I told you, Antonio shall be bound.

Shylock   *Antonio shall become bound*; well?

Bassanio   May you stead me? Will you pleasure me? Shall I know your answer?

纳　丽　莎	您不记得吗，姑娘，老大人在世时有一位威尼斯青年，是士子，又是战士，同一位蒙忒弗拉侯爵来到过这里。
宝　喜　霞	是的，是的，是跋萨尼奥；我想来，这是他的名字。
纳　丽　莎	正是，姑娘：我这双傻眼睛所见到的所有的人儿，就推他最值得配上一位佳人。
宝　喜　霞	我很记得他，且记得他果真值得你夸赞。

〔一仆人上。

怎么说？什么事？

仆　　人	姑娘，四位宾客来向您告别：又有第五位，摩洛哥亲王，差个使从来报信，说他的主人亲王殿下今晚上要来到。
宝　喜　霞	要是我能对这第五位宾客用同样的心情欢迎，如同我对那四位加以欢送，我会要对他的到来感到愉快：要是他有着圣人般的品德而生着一副魔鬼似的尊容，那就不如让他听我的忏悔，可不要做我的老公。来，纳丽莎。喂，你在头里走。寻芳的贵客才辞行，探美的佳宾又来临。

〔同下。

第　三　景

〔威尼斯。一广场〕
〔跋萨尼奥与夏洛克上。

夏　洛　克	三千金特格；唔。
跋萨尼奥	呃，朝奉，三个月为期。
夏　洛　克	三个月为期，唔。
跋萨尼奥	这笔款子，我对你说过，由安东尼奥出立借据。
夏　洛　克	由安东尼奥出立借据；唔。
跋萨尼奥	你能否助我一臂之力？你能满足我吗？你能给我个答复吗？

Shylock   Three thousand ducats, for three months, and Antonio bound.

Bassanio   Your answer to that.

Shylock   Antonio is a good man.

Bassanio   Have you heard any imputation to the contrary?

Shylock   Ho, no, no, no, no: my meaning in saying he is a good man is to have you understand me that he is sufficient; yet his means are in supposition: he hath an argosy bound to Tripolis, another to the Indies; I understand, moreover, upon the Rialto, he hath a third at Mexico, a fourth for England, and other ventures he hath, squandered abroad. But ships are but boards, sailors but men; there be land-rats and water-rats, land-thieves and water-thieves, — I mean pirates, — and then there is the peril of waters, winds, and rocks. The man is, notwithstanding, sufficient. Three thousand ducats- I think I may take his bond.

Bassanio   Be assured you may.

Shylock   I will be assured I may; and, that I may be assured, I will bethink me. May I speak with Antonio?

Bassanio   If it please you to dine with us.

Shylock   Yes, to smell pork; to eat of the habitation which your prophet, the Nazarite, conjured the devil into. I will buy with you, sell with you, talk with you, walk with you, and so following; but I will not eat with you, drink with you, nor pray with you. What news on the Rialto? Who is he comes here?

[*Enter* Antonio]

Bassanio   This is Signior Antonio.

Shylock   [*Aside.*] How like a fawning publican he looks!
I hate him for he is a Christian;
But more for that in low simplicity
He lends out money gratis, and brings down
The rate of usance here with us in Venice.
If I can catch him once upon the hip,
I will feed fat the ancient grudge I bear him.
He hates our sacred nation; and he rails,
Even there where merchants most do congregate,

夏　洛　克　三千金特格,三个月为期,安东尼奥出立借据。

跋萨尼奥　等你的答复。

夏　洛　克　安东尼奥是个好人。

跋萨尼奥　你听见过相反的责难吗?

夏　洛　克　啊,不不不:我说他是个好人,意思是要你知道,我认为他是殷实的。可是他的资产是不稳定的:他有一艘海舶开往屈黎波里,又一艘开往西印度群岛;此外,我在市场上了解到他还有第三艘在墨西哥,第四艘驶向英格兰,他还有别的风险浪掷在海上。但是船舶不过是木板,水手不过是人儿:而岸上和水上有旱老鼠和水老鼠,水贼和旱贼,我是说海盗,而此外还有水、风和礁石的危险。虽然如此,他这人还殷实。三千金特格,我想我可以接受他的借据。

跋萨尼奥　放心,你可以。

夏　洛　克　我要得到保证才可以接受;为了能得保证,我要考虑一下。我能跟安东尼奥谈谈吗?

跋萨尼奥　假如你高兴同我们一起吃饭。

夏　洛　克　是啊,去嗅猪肉味儿;去吃那个你们的先知基督把魔鬼咒进去居住的肉身。我可以跟你们做买卖,跟你们谈话和散步,等等,可是我不能同你们一起吃饭,喝酒,祈祷。市场上有什么消息? 是谁来到了这里?

　　　　　　　［安东尼奥上。

跋萨尼奥　这就是安东尼奥舍人。

夏　洛　克　［旁白］他多么像个谄媚奉承的店主人!
　　　　　　我恨他,因为他是个基督教徒,
　　　　　　但是更为了他做人非常愚蠢,
　　　　　　借钱出去不取利,因而压低了
　　　　　　我们在威城放债营生的利率。
　　　　　　若是有一天我把他压倒在地,
　　　　　　我定要深深报复我对他的宿恨。
　　　　　　他仇视我们的神圣民族,且在那
　　　　　　百行商贾汇集的场所当众

On me, my bargains, and my well-won thrift,
Which he calls interest. Cursed be my tribe
If I forgive him!

Bassanio   Shylock, do you hear?

Shylock   I am debating of my present store,
And, by the near guess of my memory,
I cannot instantly raise up the gross
Of full three thousand ducats. What of that?
Tubal, a wealthy Hebrew of my tribe,
Will furnish me. But soft! how many months
Do you desire? [*To* Antonio] Rest you fair, good signior;
Your worship was the last man in our mouths.

Antonio   Shylock, albeit I neither lend nor borrow
By taking nor by giving of excess,
Yet, to supply the ripe wants of my friend,
I'll break a custom. [*To* Bassanio] Is he yet possess'd
How much ye would?

Shylock   Ay, ay, three thousand ducats.

Antonio   And for three months.

Shylock   I had forgot; three months; you told me so.
Well then, your bond; and, let me see. But hear you,
Methought you said you neither lend nor borrow
Upon advantage.

Antonio   I do never use it.

Shylock   When Jacob graz'd his uncle Laban's sheep, —
This Jacob from our holy Abram was,
As his wise mother wrought in his behalf,
The third possessor; ay, he was the third, —

Antonio   And what of him? Did he take interest?

Shylock   No, not take interest; not, as you would say,
Directly interest; mark what Jacob did.
When Laban and himself were compromis'd
That all the eanlings which were streak'd and pied

辱骂我,鄙蔑我的交易和利润,
他叫作利息。我若原谅他,绝灭
我的种族!

跋萨尼奥　　　　　　　夏洛克,你听到没有?
夏　洛　克　我正在考虑我手头所有的现款,
据我大体上记得起来的总数,
我一时筹不到三千。但那有何妨!
我犹太同族有一位财东屠勃尔,
能供应给我。但且慢! 为期几个月,
您想要借用? ［对安］您好,祝福您,舍人,
我们适才正在交谈起您尊驾。

安东尼奥　　夏洛克,虽然我不论出借或告贷,
从不多收回或者多付出少许,
但为了我这位朋友的紧急需要,
我将破一次惯例。他知道没有,
你需要多少?

夏　洛　克　　　　　　　唔唔,三千金特格。
安东尼奥　借期三个月。
夏　洛　克　我把它忘了;三个月;您告诉过我。
好吧,您立约;我来瞧;可是您听着;
我以为您说过您借出或者告贷,
从来不收付盈余。

安东尼奥　　　　　　　　我从来不收付。
夏　洛　克　当雅各替他舅父莱朋牧羊时——
这位雅各从我们的圣祖亚伯兰
算起,他聪明的母亲为他设法,
当上了第三代族长;哦,他是的——
安东尼奥　为什么说起他? 他可收取利息吗?
夏　洛　克　不曾,没有取利息;不收取,您叫做
直接的利息:听着,雅各怎么办。
当莱朋跟雅各共同商议定当了,
出生的小羊儿,凡是有条纹斑驳的,

Should fall as Jacob's hire, the ewes, being rank,
In end of autumn turned to the rams;
And when the work of generation was
Between these woolly breeders in the act,
The skilful shepherd peel'd me certain wands,
And, in the doing of the deed of kind,
He stuck them up before the fulsome ewes,
Who, then conceiving, did in eaning time
Fall parti-colour'd lambs, and those were Jacob's.
This was a way to thrive, and he was blest;
And thrift is blessing, if men steal it not.

Antonio   This was a venture, sir, that Jacob serv'd for;
A thing not in his power to bring to pass,
But sway'd and fashion'd by the hand of heaven.
Was this inserted to make interest good?
Or is your gold and silver ewes and rams?

Shylock   I cannot tell; I make it breed as fast.
But note me, signior.

Antonio   Mark you this, Bassanio,
The devil can cite Scripture for his purpose.
An evil soul producing holy witness
Is like a villain with a smiling cheek,
A goodly apple rotten at the heart.
O, what a goodly outside falsehood hath!

Shylock   Three thousand ducats; 'tis a good round sum.
Three months from twelve; then let me see the rate.

Antonio   Well, Shylock, shall we be beholding to you?

Shylock   Signior Antonio, many a time and oft
In the Rialto you have rated me
About my moneys and my usances;
Still have I borne it with a patient shrug,
For suff'rance is the badge of all our tribe;
You call me misbeliever, cut-throat dog,

　　　　　　　　归雅各所有,作为工资;秋末时,
　　　　　　　　那些母羊,因情欲发作,跟公羊
　　　　　　　　交配,而当传种的动作正好在
　　　　　　　　这些毛茸畜生间进行的当儿,
　　　　　　　　这机灵的牧人剥了些树枝的皮,
　　　　　　　　插在发浪的母羊跟前泥土中,
　　　　　　　　这些受孕的母羊产下羊仔来,
　　　　　　　　凡是斑条羊就都归雅各所有。
　　　　　　　　这是繁昌的道路,而他是得福的,
　　　　　　　　繁荣昌盛是福佑,只要不偷盗。

安 东 尼 奥　　这是雅各所追随的机运,朝奉;
　　　　　　　　但成就与否不在他掌握之中,
　　　　　　　　而是由上天的意趣所支配和形成。
　　　　　　　　你说这件事,可是说取利是好事?
　　　　　　　　或者说你的金钱是公羊和母羊?

夏 洛 克　　那可说不上;我使它孳生得快,
　　　　　　　　听我说,老舍人。

安 东 尼 奥　　　　　　　　你瞧,跋萨尼奥,
　　　　　　　　魔鬼为他的目的,能征引圣经。
　　　　　　　　一个罪恶的灵魂用圣洁的凭证,
　　　　　　　　好比是一名呈露笑脸的恶棍,
　　　　　　　　一只穿心腐烂的美好的苹果:
　　　　　　　　啊,欺诈有多么美好的表象!

夏 洛 克　　三千金特格;这是一大笔整数。
　　　　　　　　十二分之三;我来看,有多少;利率——

安 东 尼 奥　　好了,夏洛克,我们能否指望你?

夏 洛 克　　安东尼奥舍人,不知有多少回
　　　　　　　　您在市场上对我的款项和利润
　　　　　　　　总是频施诋毁和粗野的辱骂:
　　　　　　　　我总是耐心地耸一耸肩忍受,
　　　　　　　　因逆来顺受是我们族类的标识。
　　　　　　　　您谩骂我是邪教徒,凶残的恶狗,

And spet upon my Jewish gaberdine,
And all for use of that which is mine own.
Well then, it now appears you need my help;
Go to, then; you come to me, and you say
Shylock, we would have moneys. You say so:
You that did void your rheum upon my beard,
And foot me as you spurn a stranger cur
Over your threshold; moneys is your suit.
What should I say to you? Should I not say
Hath a dog money? Is it possible
A cur can lend three thousand ducats? Or
Shall I bend low and, in a bondman's key,
With bated breath and whisp'ring humbleness,
Say this: —
Fair sir, you spit on me on Wednesday last;
You spurn'd me such a day; another time
You call'd me dog; and for these courtesies
I'll lend you thus much moneys?

Antonio   I am as like to call thee so again,
To spet on thee again, to spurn thee too.
If thou wilt lend this money, lend it not
As to thy friends, — for when did friendship take
A breed for barren metal of his friend? —
But lend it rather to thine enemy;
Who if he break thou mayst with better face
Exact the penalty.

Shylock   Why, look you, how you storm!
I would be friends with you, and have your love,
Forget the shames that you have stain'd me with,
Supply your present wants, and take no doit
Of usance for my moneys, and you'll not hear me:
This is kind I offer.

Bassanio   This were kindness.

　　　　　　　　把唾沫吐在我的犹太外套上，
　　　　　　　　只因我使用了自己的款子作经营。
　　　　　　　　很好，看来您现在需要我帮忙：
　　　　　　　　得了，那么；您跑来找我，并且说
　　　　　　　　"夏洛克，我们要用款子"：您说道；
　　　　　　　　您啊，曾把唾沫吐在我须髯上，
　　　　　　　　用脚踢我，像踢您那门槛外边
　　　　　　　　一条野狗：借款子是您的恳求。
　　　　　　　　我应该对您说什么？我应否说道，
　　　　　　　　"一条狗能有钱吗？是不是可能
　　　　　　　　一条狗能够贷出三千元?"或者，
　　　　　　　　我应当弯下身子，用奴才的调门，
　　　　　　　　屏息而低声，恭而敬之地说道：
　　　　　　　　"好大爷，上个星期三您吐我唾沫；
　　　　　　　　某一天您用脚踢我；又有一回
　　　　　　　　您叫我狗子；为了这些个殷勤，
　　　　　　　　我要借给您如许钱款?"

安 东 尼 奥　　我很有可能再这样叫你骂你，
　　　　　　　　再吐你唾沫，再像往常般踢你。
　　　　　　　　你若是肯借这笔钱，不必借贷给
　　　　　　　　你的朋友；因为友谊怎么会
　　　　　　　　从朋友那儿收取硬金银的子息？
　　　　　　　　你若借贷，就作为借给你的仇人，
　　　　　　　　他呀，假使他失约，你更好便于
　　　　　　　　按立约处罚。

夏 洛 克　　　　　　　　　哎哟，您的气好大！
　　　　　　　　我心想跟您攀交情，得您的友好，
　　　　　　　　忘记您过去对我的种种羞辱，
　　　　　　　　供应您目前的需要而不收一分钱
　　　　　　　　作为我款子的息金，可是您不听：
　　　　　　　　我完全是一片好意。

跋 萨 尼 奥　　这真像是好意。

Shylock   This kindness will I show.

Go with me to a notary, seal me there

Your single bond; and, in a merry sport,

If you repay me not on such a day,

In such a place, such sum or sums as are

Express'd in the condition, let the forfeit

Be nominated for an equal pound

Of your fair flesh, to be cut off and taken

In what part of your body pleaseth me.

Antonio   Content, in faith; I'll seal to such a bond,

And say there is much kindness in the Jew.

Bassanio   You shall not seal to such a bond for me;

I'll rather dwell in my necessity.

Antonio   Why, fear not, man; I will not forfeit it;

Within these two months, that's a month before

This bond expires, I do expect return

Of thrice three times the value of this bond.

Shylock   O father Abram, what these Christians are,

Whose own hard dealings teaches them suspect

The thoughts of others. Pray you, tell me this;

If he should break his day, what should I gain

By the exaction of the forfeiture?

A pound of man's flesh, taken from a man,

Is not so estimable, profitable neither,

As flesh of muttons, beefs, or goats. I say,

To buy his favour, I extend this friendship;

If he will take it, so; if not, adieu;

And, for my love, I pray you wrong me not.

Antonio   Yes, Shylock, I will seal unto this bond.

Shylock   Then meet me forthwith at the notary's;

Give him direction for this merry bond,

And I will go and purse the ducats straight,

夏　洛　克　　　　　　　　这好意我要表示。
　　　　　　　同我去找个公证人，就在他那儿
　　　　　　　签好了单独债券；为了当作玩，
　　　　　　　您在某月某日，某一个地点，
　　　　　　　不归还我契据里写明的如许
　　　　　　　如许数目，让罚则定会在您
　　　　　　　身体上不论哪一处，随我的高兴，
　　　　　　　割下整整一磅白肉来作抵偿。

安东尼奥　我满意，当真；我要签这个借据，
　　　　　　　而说这个犹太人对我很善意。

跋萨尼奥　你绝不可以为我签这个债券：
　　　　　　　我宁愿没有这笔款子而落空。

安东尼奥　嗨，老弟，别害怕；我不会受罚，
　　　　　　　这两个月内，在这债券到期前
　　　　　　　一个月，我指望有这债券上的数目
　　　　　　　三倍又三倍，回归到我这手里来。

夏　洛　克　啊，亚伯兰始祖，这些基督徒
　　　　　　　怎么这模样，他们自己太苛刻，
　　　　　　　倒怀疑人家的善意！请您告诉我，
　　　　　　　如果他到期失约，我有何好处，
　　　　　　　按照借据上规定的条款取罚？
　　　　　　　从一个人身上割下一磅人肉，
　　　　　　　比起胡羊肉、牛肉、山羊肉来，
　　　　　　　还不那么样值钱或有利。我说，
　　　　　　　为博取他的好感，我豁出这友情：
　　　　　　　他若是接受，那就好；否则，再会；
　　　　　　　对我的友好，请您切莫要唐突。

安东尼奥　好的，夏洛克，我要签署这债券。

夏　洛　克　那么，就请到公证人那里碰头；
　　　　　　　关照他怎样订立这玩笑的借据，
　　　　　　　我要马上去把款子装入钱囊，
　　　　　　　还要回家去照顾一下，留给了

See to my house, left in the fearful guard
Of an unthrifty knave, and presently
I'll be with you.
Antonio   Hie thee, gentle Jew.

[*Exit* Shylock.]

This Hebrew will turn Christian: he grows kind.
Bassanio   I like not fair terms and a villain's mind.
Antonio   Come on; in this there can be no dismay;
My ships come home a month before the day.

[*Exeunt.*]

　　　　　一个烂污的奴才去守护不放心，
　　　　　接着便赶来找你们。
安 东 尼 奥　　你赶快，温存的犹太人。

　　　　　　　　　　　　　　　　　　　　［夏洛克下。

　　　　　这个犹太人就要成为基督徒：
　　　　　他变得善良了。
跋 萨 尼 奥　　　　　　　我不爱口蜜腹剑。
安 东 尼 奥　别着慌：这件事没有什么可低徊；
　　　　　到期前一个月，我的船都会回港来。

　　　　　　　　　　　　　　　　　　　　［同下。

ACT II.

SCENE I. Belmont. *A room in* Portia's *house.*

[*Flourish of cornets. Enter the* Prince of Morocco, *and his Followers*;
Portia, Nerissa, and Others attending.]

Prince of Morocco   Mislike me not for my complexion,
The shadow'd livery of the burnish'd sun,
To whom I am a neighbour, and near bred.
Bring me the fairest creature northward born,
Where Phoebus' fire scarce thaws the icicles,
And let us make incision for your love
To prove whose blood is reddest, his or mine.
I tell thee, lady, this aspect of mine
Hath fear'd the valiant; by my love, I swear
The best-regarded virgins of our clime
Have lov'd it too. I would not change this hue,
Except to steal your thoughts, my gentle queen.

Portia   In terms of choice I am not solely led
By nice direction of a maiden's eyes;
Besides, the lottery of my destiny
Bars me the right of voluntary choosing;
But, if my father had not scanted me

第 二 幕

第 一 景

［贝尔蒙。宝喜霞邸内一室］

［长鸣齐奏。摩洛哥亲王率扈从上，喜宝霞、纳丽莎
及仆从随侍。

摩 洛 哥　莫要因我的容颜而对我嫌厌，
　　　　　这是熠熠阳乌的晦闇的公服，
　　　　　它啊，我是它邻曲和相近的亲人。
　　　　　跟我在北国找个最白皙的人来，
　　　　　那里费勃斯的火焰难得化垂冰，
　　　　　让我们契血来验证对您的情愫，
　　　　　比一比是他的，还是我的最殷红。
　　　　　告诉您，姑娘，我这副相貌曾使
　　　　　骁勇者胆怯：凭我的爱情，我起誓，
　　　　　我们疆土上最被尊崇的处女
　　　　　都曾爱过它：我不愿变易这色泽，
　　　　　温良的女王，除了为吸引您的喜爱。

宝 喜 霞　要获致雀屏中选，并不取决于
　　　　　一位窈窕淑女的微妙的眼光；
　　　　　而况，我相从与否这命运的拈阄，
　　　　　摒绝了我的自愿取舍的主权：
　　　　　但如果我父亲未曾以他的灵明

And hedg'd me by his wit, to yield myself
His wife who wins me by that means I told you,
Yourself, renowned Prince, then stood as fair
As any comer I have look'd on yet
For my affection.

Prince of Morocco   Even for that I thank you:
Therefore, I pray you, lead me to the caskets
To try my fortune. By this scimitar, —
That slew the Sophy and a Persian prince,
That won three fields of Sultan Solyman, —
I would o'erstare the sternest eyes that look,
Outbrave the heart most daring on the earth,
Pluck the young sucking cubs from the she-bear,
Yea, mock the lion when he roars for prey,
To win thee, lady. But, alas the while!
If Hercules and Lichas play at dice
Which is the better man, the greater throw
May turn by fortune from the weaker hand:
So is Alcides beaten by his page;
And so may I, blind Fortune leading me,
Miss that which one unworthier may attain,
And die with grieving.

Portia   You must take your chance,
And either not attempt to choose at all,
Or swear before you choose, if you choose wrong,
Never to speak to lady afterward
In way of marriage; therefore be advis'd.

Prince of Morocco   Nor will not; come, bring me unto my
        chance.

Portia   First, forward to the temple: after dinner
Your hazard shall be made.

限制、拦阻我，我要嫁哪位君子，
匹配我他得遵循我告您的程序，
那么，您殿下，声名赫奕的亲王，
在我看来便跟不论哪一位
来访的君侯同样地修美，同样
值得我恩爱。

摩 洛 哥　　　　　　就为这一层，感谢您；
因而，请您领我到匣儿那里去，
去试探我的命运。我凭这弯刀
起誓，它斩过波斯王和一位三次
战败过索列曼苏丹的波斯亲王，
我要怒目瞪退最威武的雄杰，
威震这世上人间最勇猛的英豪，
从母熊胸头拉下给喂奶的子熊，
哎，当一头饿狮咆哮时嘲弄它，
为求得您的情爱。但是，唉呀！
赫居里若跟他的侍从列却斯掷骰
赌赛比高低，大点子也许碰运气
会出自那无力小子轻挥的手中：
于是大力神便这般给僮儿所败；
这样，我也许被盲目的逆运所引领
失掉了机缘，给不堪的庸人所得，
而在悲伤里丧命。

宝 喜 霞　　　　　　　您得凭命运，
或者放弃掉，不再企图去挑选，
否则挑选之前立下誓，挑错了
决不再向哪一位姑娘求婚配：
故而要请您考虑。

摩 洛 哥　　　　　　我不会。来吧，
引我去试探命运。

宝 喜 霞　　　　　首先，到庙里：
午餐后您将去冒险。

Prince of Morocco Good fortune then!
To make me blest or cursed'st among men!

[*Cornets, and exeunt.*]

SCENE II. Venice. *A street*

[*Enter* Launcelot.]

Launcelot Certainly my conscience will serve me to run
from this Jew my master. The fiend is at mine elbow
and tempts me, saying to me *Gobbo*, *Launcelot Gobbo*,
good Launcelot or *good Gobbo* or *good Launcelot Gobbo*,
use your legs, *take the start*, *run away*. My conscience says *No*; *take heed*, *honest Launcelot*, *take
heed*, *honest Gobbo* or, as aforesaid, *honest Launcelot
Gobbo*, *do not run*; *scorn running with thy heels*.
Well, the most courageous fiend bids me pack. *Via!*
says the fiend; *away!* says the fiend. *For the heavens*, *rouse up a brave mind*, says the fiend *and run*.
Well, my conscience, hanging about the neck of my
heart, says very wisely to me *My honest friend
Launcelot*, *being an honest man's son* — or rather an
honest woman's son; — for indeed my father did
something smack, something grow to, he had a kind
of taste; — well, my conscience says *Launcelot*,
budge not. *Budge*, says the fiend. *Budge not*, says
my conscience. *Conscience*, say I, you counsel well.
Fiend, say I, *you counsel well*. To be ruled by my
conscience, I should stay with the Jew my master,
who, God bless the mark! is a kind of devil; and, to
run away from the Jew, I should be ruled by the
fiend, who, saving your reverence! is the devil himself. Certainly the Jew is the very devil incarnal; and,
in my conscience, my conscience is but a kind of hard
conscience, to offer to counsel me to stay with the
Jew. The fiend gives the more friendly counsel: I will
run, fiend; my heels are at your commandment; I will
run.

[*Enter Old* Gobbo, *with a basket.*]

摩 洛 哥 　　　　　　　愿好运来临!

我或者成功得福,或失败而丧命。

　　　　　　　　　　　　　　　　　[长鸣齐奏,同下。

第 二 景

[威尼斯。一街道]

[朗斯洛忒上。

朗斯洛忒　当然,我的良心会同意我从这犹太主人家里逃走。
魔鬼在我的臂肘旁引诱我,说道,"高卜,朗斯洛
忒·高卜,好朗斯洛忒",或是"好高卜",或是"好朗
斯洛忒·高卜,使用你的腿儿,就开始吧,跑掉"。我
的良心说,"不要;注意,老实的朗斯洛忒;注意,老实
的高卜,"或是,如刚才所说,"老实的朗斯洛忒·高
卜;别跑;鄙视用你的脚跟逃跑。"好,那个挺大胆的
魔鬼叫我收拾行李:"上路!"魔鬼道;"走啊!"魔鬼
道;"为了老天,鼓起胆来,"魔鬼道,"就跑。"好,我的
良心挂在我心儿的脖子上,很聪明地对我说,"我的
老实朋友朗斯洛忒,是个老实人的儿子,"或许该说
是个老实妇人的儿子;因为,老实讲,我父亲有点儿
气味,有点儿那个,他有一种味儿;好,我的良心说,
"朗斯洛忒,别动。""动,"魔鬼说。"别动,"我的良心
说。"良心,"我说道,"你出的主意对;""魔鬼,"我说
道,"你出的主意对;"依了我的良心,我该待在我的
犹太主人这里,他啊,上帝恕我,是个魔鬼;而从犹太
人这里逃跑,我就会跟着魔鬼跑,他啊,对不起,本身
就是魔鬼。这犹太人肯定是魔鬼的化身;而我这良
心,凭良心讲,是个硬良心,因为它出主意,叫我待在
这犹太人这里。魔鬼替我出的主意倒比较友好:我
决计逃跑,魔鬼;我的脚跟听从你的指挥;我要跑。

　　　　　　　[老高卜携篮上。

Gobbo   Master young man, you, I pray you; which is the
way to Master Jew's?

Launcelot   [*Aside.*] O heavens! This is my true-begotten
father, who, being more than sand-blind, high-gravel
blind, knows me not: I will try confusions with him.

Gobbo   Master young gentleman, I pray you, which is the
way to Master Jew's?

Launcelot   Turn up on your right hand at the next turning, but, at the next turning of all, on your left;
marry, at the very next turning, turn of no hand, but
turn down indirectly to the Jew's house.

Gobbo   Be God's sonties, 'twill be a hard way to hit. Can
you tell me whether one Launcelot, that dwells with
him, dwell with him or no?

Launcelot   Talk you of young Master Launcelot?
[*Aside.*] Mark me now; now will I raise the waters.
Talk you of young Master Launcelot?

Gobbo   No master, sir, but a poor man's son; his father,
though I say't, is an honest exceeding poor man, and,
God be thanked, well to live.

Launcelot   Well, let his father be what 'a will, we talk of
young Master Launcelot.

Gobbo   Your worship's friend, and Launcelot, sir.

Launcelot   But I pray you, ergo, old man, ergo, I beseech you, talk you of young Master Launcelot?

Gobbo   Of Launcelot, an't please your mastership.

Launcelot   Ergo, Master Launcelot. Talk not of Master
Launcelot, father; for the young gentleman, — according to Fates and Destinies and such odd sayings,
the Sisters Three and such branches of learning, — is
indeed deceased; or, as you would say in plain terms,
gone to heaven.

Gobbo   Marry, God forbid! The boy was the very staff of
my age, my very prop.

Launcelot   Do I look like a cudgel or a hovel-post, a staff
or a prop? Do you know me, father?

Gobbo   Alack the day! I know you not, young gentleman;
but I pray you tell me, is my boy — God rest his
soul! —alive or dead?

Launcelot   Do you not know me, father?

Gobbo   Alack, sir, I am sand-blind; I know you not.

高　　卜	小官人,您,请问您,到犹太老板家怎么走?
朗斯洛忒	〔旁白〕天啊,这是我亲生老子! 他的眼睛比沙盲还厉害,是石子盲,认不得我;我来逗着他玩儿。
高　　卜	小官人,年轻的士子,请问您,到犹太老板家怎么走?
朗斯洛忒	下一个拐弯你往右手拐,最后一个拐弯你往左边拐;凭圣母,就在下一个拐弯不用拐,便直接到了犹太老板家。
高　　卜	上帝可怜见,这可难找了。您可能告诉我,有一个朗斯洛忒待在他那儿,可还待在他那儿不。
朗斯洛忒	你是讲的朗斯洛忒小官人吗?〔旁白〕瞧着我来叫他流些眼水。你是说的朗斯洛忒小官人吗?
高　　卜	不是小官人,小官人,只是个穷人的儿子:他老子,我虽然这么说,是个老实的贫寒透顶的人儿,不过多谢上帝,还活得不错。
朗斯洛忒	得,由他的老子去要怎样便怎样,咱们讲的是年轻的朗斯洛忒小官人。
高　　卜	您官人的朋友,他叫朗斯洛忒,小官人。
朗斯洛忒	可是我来问你,故而,老人,故而,我求你,你讲的可是朗斯洛忒小官人?
高　　卜	是朗斯洛忒,要是您小官人高兴。
朗斯洛忒	故而,朗斯洛忒小官人。别说朗斯洛忒小官人了,老人家;因为这年轻的士子,根据运命、气数和这一类怪异的说法,三姐妹那等方术,是当真去世了,或者如你用常言来说的,叫做归了天。
高　　卜	凭圣母,上帝不准! 这孩子是我老来的拐棍,我的依仗啊。
朗斯洛忒	我看来像根棒头或撑柱,一根拐棍或支杖吗? 你认识我吗,老人家?
高　　卜	唉呀,我不认识,年轻的士予;可是,我求您,告诉我,我的孩子,上帝安息他的灵魂,是活着还是死了?
朗斯洛忒	你不认识我吗,老爹?
高　　卜	唉,小官人,我是个沙盲瞎子;我不认识您。

Launcelot Nay, indeed, if you had your eyes, you might fail of the knowing me: it is a wise father that knows his own child. Well, old man, I will tell you news of your son. Give me your blessing; truth will come to light; murder cannot be hid long; a man's son may, but in the end truth will out.

Gobbo Pray you, sir, stand up; I am sure you are not Launcelot, my boy.

Launcelot Pray you, let's have no more fooling about it, but give me your blessing; I am Launcelot, your boy that was, your son that is, your child that shall be.

Gobbo I cannot think you are my son.

Launcelot I know not what I shall think of that; but I am Launcelot, the Jew's man, and I am sure Margery your wife is my mother.

Gobbo Her name is Margery, indeed: I'll be sworn, if thou be Launcelot, thou art mine own flesh and blood. Lord worshipped might he be, what a beard hast thou got! Thou hast got more hair on thy chin than Dobbin my thill-horse has on his tail.

Launcelot It should seem, then, that Dobbin's tail grows backward; I am sure he had more hair on his tail than I have on my face when I last saw him.

Gobbo Lord! how art thou changed! How dost thou and thy master agree? I have brought him a present. How gree you now?

Launcelot Well, well; but, for mine own part, as I have set up my rest to run away, so I will not rest till I have run some ground. My master's a very Jew. Give him a present! Give him a halter. I am famished in his service; you may tell every finger I have with my ribs. Father, I am glad you are come; give me your present to one Master Bassanio, who indeed gives rare new liveries. If I serve not him, I will run as far as God has any ground. O rare fortune! Here comes the man: to him, father; for I am a Jew, if I serve the Jew any longer.

朗斯洛忒	不认识,当真,要是你眼睛不坏,你也不见得会认识我:得有个聪明老子才能认识他自己的儿子。好吧,老人家,我来告诉你你儿子的消息:祝福我:真相会显露出来;谋杀不能隐藏得太久;一个人儿的儿子也许能躲避一时,可是事实终于会显露。
高　卜	请您,小官人,站直了:我相信您不是朗斯洛忒我的孩子。
朗斯洛忒	我们别再瞎胡闹了,请你给我祝福吧:我是朗斯洛忒,过去是你的孩子,现在是你的儿子,将来是你的小子。
高　卜	我不能相信你是我的儿子。
朗斯洛忒	我不知道我该有个怎样的想法:可是我确实是朗斯洛忒,犹太人雇的小厮,我也确实知道你的老婆玛吉蕾是我的妈。
高　卜	她名叫玛吉蕾,不错:我可以赌咒,你若是朗斯洛忒,你就是咱的亲生骨肉了。上帝委实是圣灵!你脸上长得好一把须髯啊!你下巴上长的毛比我那驾车的马儿道平拖的尾巴还多。
朗斯洛忒	那么,看来是道平的尾巴倒着长了:我蛮有把握;我最后见到它时,它的尾巴毛长得比我现在脸上的毛多得多哩。
高　卜	上帝啊,你变得多厉害!你跟你主人合得来吗?我给他带了件礼物来。你们合得来吗?
朗斯洛忒	得了,得了;可是,拿我来说,我既然已经决计逃跑,我就非跑它一程路决不会停下来。我这主人是个十足的犹太佬:给他一件礼物!给他一根绳子去上吊:我替他干活挨饿;你能用我的每一根手指去数我的肋骨。阿爸,你看我很高兴:你替我把礼物送给跋萨尼奥官人,他啊,当真的,把漂亮的新制服给仆人穿:我若不侍候他,我要跑遍这世界。啊,好运道!这来的就是他,爸爸;我若再侍候那犹太佬,我就是个犹太人。

[*Enter* Bassanio, *with* Leonardo, *with and other* Followers.

Bassanio You may do so; but let it be so hasted that supper be ready at the farthest by five of the clock. See
these letters delivered, put the liveries to making,
and desire Gratiano to come anon to my lodging.

[*Exit a* Servant.]

Launcelot To him, father.

Gobbo God bless your worship!

Bassanio Gramercy; wouldst thou aught with me?

Gobbo Here's my son, sir, a poor boy—

Launcelot Not a poor boy, sir, but the rich Jew's man,
that would, sir, — as my father shall specify—

Gobbo He hath a great infection, sir, as one would say,
to serve—

Launcelot Indeed the short and the long is, I serve the Jew,
and have a desire, as my father shall specify—

Gobbo His master and he, saving your worship's reverence, are scarce cater-cousins—

Launcelot To be brief, the very truth is that the Jew, having done me wrong, doth cause me, — as my father, being I hope an old man, shall frutify unto you—

Gobbo I have here a dish of doves that I would bestow
upon your worship; and my suit is—

Launcelot In very brief, the suit is impertinent to myself,
as your worship shall know by this honest old man;
and, though I say it, though old man, yet poor man,
my father.

Bassanio One speak for both. What would you?

Launcelot Serve you, sir.

Gobbo That is the very defect of the matter, sir.

Bassanio I know thee well; thou hast obtain'd thy suit. Shylock thy master spoke with me this day, And hath preferr'd
thee, if it be preferment To leave a rich Jew's service to become The follower of so poor a gentleman.

Launcelot The old proverb is very well parted between
my master Shylock and you, sir: you have the grace
of God, sir, and he hath enough.

〔跋萨尼奥与里奥哪铎及其他从人上。

跋 萨 尼 奥　你可以这么办；可是得赶快，晚饭最晚要在五点钟准
　　　　　　备好。这几封信送掉；把制服裁做起来，请葛拉希阿
　　　　　　诺马上到我寓所来。
　　　　　　　　　　　　　　　　〔一仆人下。

朗 斯 洛 忒　上前，爸爸。
高　　　卜　上帝保佑大官人！
跋 萨 尼 奥　多谢你，有什么事？
高　　　卜　这是我的儿子，大官人，一个可怜的孩子，——
朗 斯 洛 忒　不是个可怜孩子，大官人，是那犹太财东的小厮；我
　　　　　　愿意，大官人，我爸爸会告诉您——
高　　　卜　他有个大缺点，大官人，正如人家说的，来侍候，——
朗 斯 洛 忒　果然，总而言之，我侍候那犹太人，如今想要，我爸爸
　　　　　　会详细——
高　　　卜　他主人跟他，不瞒您大官人说，有点儿合不拢来——
朗 斯 洛 忒　干脆说一句，事实是那犹太人，给我吃了苦头，使得
　　　　　　我，我爸爸，他是，我希望，一个老头儿，会向您
　　　　　　陈明——
高　　　卜　我这里有一盘烤好的鸽子愿意奉送给大官人，我要
　　　　　　请求的是——
朗 斯 洛 忒　简单道来，这请求不关我自己，您大官人会从这老实
　　　　　　的老人家这里得知；所以，我虽是这么说，他虽是个
　　　　　　老人，可是个穷人，我爸爸。
跋 萨 尼 奥　由一个人讲。你们要什么？
朗 斯 洛 忒　侍候您，大官人。
高　　　卜　那正是这事情的缺点，大官人。
跋 萨 尼 奥　我很认得你；我答允你的要求：
　　　　　　你主人夏洛克今儿跟我谈过，
　　　　　　把你荐升给了我，假使你离开
　　　　　　一个犹太财东，来当这样穷
　　　　　　一个士子的从人，能叫做荐升。
朗 斯 洛 忒　一句老话一分为二正好应在我主人夏洛克和您身
　　　　　　上，大官人：您有了上帝的神恩，他有的是钱。

Bassanio Thou speak'st it well. Go, father, with thy son.
Take leave of thy old master, and inquire
My lodging out. [*To a Servant*] Give him a livery
More guarded than his fellows'; see it done.

Launcelot Father, in. I cannot get a service, no! I have
ne'er a tongue in my head! [*Looking on his palm*] Well;
if any man in Italy have a fairer table which doth offer to
swear upon a book, I shall have good fortune. Go to;
here's a simple line of life: here's a small trifle of wives;
alas, fifteen wives is nothing; a'leven widows and nine
maids is a simple coming-in for one man. And then to
scape drowning thrice, and to be in peril of my life with
the edge of a feather-bed; here are simple 'scapes. Well,
if Fortune be a woman, she's a good wench for this gear.
Father, come; I'll take my leave of the Jew in the twin-
kling of an eye.

[*Exeunt* Launcelot *and Old* Gobbo.]

Bassanio I pray thee, good Leonardo, think on this:
These things being bought and orderly bestow'd,
Return in haste, for I do feast to-night
My best esteem'd acquaintance; hie thee, go.

Leonardo My best endeavours shall be done herein.

[*Enter* Gratiano.]

Gratiano Where's your master?

Leonardo   Yonder, sir, he walks.

[*Exit.*]

Gratiano Signior Bassanio!

Bassanio Gratiano!

Gratiano I have suit to you.

Bassanio   You have obtain'd it.

Gratiano You must not deny me: I must go with you to
Belmont.

Bassanio Why, then you must. But hear thee, Gratiano;
Thou art too wild, too rude, and bold of voice;
Parts that become thee happily enough,

跋萨尼奥 你说得利落。同你的儿子，老人家，
去跟他那位旧主人道别，然后
去问明我的寓所。[向一仆人]给一套制服
与他，要比别人的显焕些：照着办。

朗斯洛忒 爸爸，里边来。不成，我弄不到一个好差事；我这脑袋里这舌头不顶事。[看着他的手掌]好啊，要是不管谁在意大利有生得比我这能按着《圣经》起誓的手掌上更好的掌纹，[我才不信呢，]我的运道是出色的。得了，这是一条单一的寿命线：这儿有不多几个老婆；哎呀，十五个老婆算不了什么；十一个寡妇和九个闺女对于一个男子汉算不了什么：还有，三次掉在水里不淹死，有一次却在鸭绒床榻边上险些儿送了命；这儿是见得能死里逃生。好吧，要是命运神是个女的，她这一着倒是个好娘儿的一着。爸爸，进来；我要花一眨眼的工夫跟那犹太老板道别。

[朗斯洛忒与老高卜下。

跋萨尼奥 我请你，好里奥哪铎，烦劳你了；
这些东西买好了，装上船以后，
赶快回来，因为我今夜要宴请
我最最尊重的朋友：请赶快，去吧。

里奥哪铎 我一定替您尽最大的努力照办。

[葛拉希阿诺上。

葛拉希阿诺 你主人在哪里？

里奥哪铎 那边，官人，散着步。 [下。

葛拉希阿诺 跋萨尼奥仁君！

跋萨尼奥 葛拉希阿诺！

葛拉希阿诺 我对您要提个要求。

跋萨尼奥 我答应了你。

葛拉希阿诺 您一定不能拒绝我；我得跟您到贝尔蒙去。

跋萨尼奥 那么，你就准定去。可是你听着，
葛拉希阿诺；你太放浪，太粗豪，
高声说话：这些个对于你很合适，

And in such eyes as ours appear not faults;
But where thou art not known, why there they show
Something too liberal. Pray thee, take pain
To allay with some cold drops of modesty
Thy skipping spirit, lest through thy wild behaviour
I be misconstrued in the place I go to,
And lose my hopes.

Gratiano   Signior Bassanio, hear me:
If I do not put on a sober habit,
Talk with respect, and swear but now and then,
Wear prayer-books in my pocket, look demurely,
Nay more, while grace is saying, hood mine eyes
Thus with my hat, and sigh, and say *amen*;
Use all the observance of civility,
Like one well studied in a sad ostent
To please his grandam, never trust me more.

Bassanio Well, we shall see your bearing.

Gratiano Nay, but I bar to-night; you shall not gauge me
By what we do to-night.

Bassanio   No, that were pity;
I would entreat you rather to put on
Your boldest suit of mirth, for we have friends
That purpose merriment. But fare you well;
I have some business.

Gratiano And I must to Lorenzo and the rest;
But we will visit you at supper-time.

[Exeunt.]

SCENE III. The same. *A room in* Shylock's *house.*

[Enter Jessica *and* Launcelot.*]*

Jessica I am sorry thou wilt leave my father so:

在我们眼里并不显得是缺点；
但在生疏的场合，那就显见得
有点儿放肆。务请你尽力设法
在你那跳跃的精神里注入几滴
冷静的谦恭，否则由于你的轻举，
我会在我的所去之处被误解，
而丧失希望。

葛拉希阿诺 　　　　　　跋萨尼奥仁君，
听我说：我倘使不罩上一层端庄，
言谈间温文尔雅，只偶然赌个咒，
袋里装着祈祷书，脸上很严肃，
还不够，餐前祷告时，把帽子压低，
遮住了眼睛，叹息着说声"阿门"，
遵循了一切谨守礼仪的风范，
像个去讨老祖父喜欢的人儿般，
装得个郁郁苍苍，就永远莫信我。

跋 萨 尼 奥 很好，我们且看你的行止吧。

葛拉希阿诺 今晚上不作数：你可别把我今天
夜里的行动来估量。

跋 萨 尼 奥 　　　　　　　　不会，那可惜：
我要请你发挥你最不羁的欢快，
因大家好友们要作乐。可是再会吧：
我有别的事。

葛拉希阿诺 我也得去找洛良佐和别的一伙：
但我们将在晚饭时和你相会。

　　　　　　　　　　　　　　　　　〔同下。

第 三 景

〔同前。夏洛克家中一室〕
〔絜雪格与朗斯洛忒上。

絜 雪 格 你这样离开我父亲，我觉得难受：

Our house is hell, and thou, a merry devil,
Didst rob it of some taste of tediousness.
But fare thee well; there is a ducat for thee;
And, Launcelot, soon at supper shalt thou see
Lorenzo, who is thy new master's guest:
Give him this letter; do it secretly.
And so farewell. I would not have my father
See me in talk with thee.

Launcelot Adieu! tears exhibit my tongue. Most beauti-
ful pagan, most sweet Jew! If a Christian do not play
the knave and get thee, I am much deceived. But, a-
dieu! these foolish drops do something drown my
manly spirit; adieu!

Jessica Farewell, good Launcelot.

[*Exit* Launcelot.]

Alack, what heinous sin is it in me
To be asham'd to be my father's child!
But though I am a daughter to his blood,
I am not to his manners. O Lorenzo!
If thou keep promise, I shall end this strife,
Become a Christian and thy loving wife.

[*Exit.*]

SCENE IV. The same. *A street*

[*Enter* Gratiano, Lorenzo,
Salarino, *and* Salanio.]

Lorenzo Nay, we will slink away in supper-time,
Disguise us at my lodging, and return
All in an hour.

Gratiano We have not made good preparation.

Salarino We have not spoke us yet of torch-bearers.

Salanio 'Tis vile, unless it may be quaintly order'd,
And better in my mind not undertook.

　　　　这个家是地狱,你是个淘气的小鬼,
　　　　破除了几分常日的无聊单调。
　　　　可是祝你好,这儿一块钱你收着:
　　　　朗斯洛忒,就在晚餐时你见到
　　　　洛良佐,他是你新主人今晚的客人:
　　　　给他这封信;悄悄地私下捎给他;
　　　　再会吧:我不愿给我爸爸见到
　　　　我在跟你说着话。

朗斯洛忒　祝平安! 眼泪替代了我的舌头。最标致的异教徒,
　　　　最温柔的犹太闺女! 若不是有个基督徒来将你骗
　　　　走,就算我太糊涂。可是,再见了:这几滴傻眼泪差
　　　　不多淹没了我的男儿气概:再会。

絮　雪　格　再会啊,好朗斯洛忒。　　　　　　　　[朗斯洛忒下。
　　　　唉哟,这真是我多么深重的罪辜,
　　　　竟会得羞于做我父亲的孩子!
　　　　可是我虽在血统上是他的女儿,
　　　　在做人行事上可不是。啊,洛良佐,
　　　　你若守信约,我将平静这心头浪,
　　　　信奉基督教,做你恩爱的好妻房。

　　　　　　　　　　　　　　　　　　　　　　　[下。

第　四　景

　　[同前。一街道]
　　[葛拉希阿诺、洛良佐、萨拉里诺与萨拉尼奥上。

洛　良　佐　且不,我们在晚餐时分溜出去,
　　　　在我寓所里化装好,然后回来,
　　　　前后一小时。

葛拉希阿诺　　　　　　　我们准备得还不够。

萨拉里诺　我们还没找好执火把的僮儿。

萨拉尼奥　那就要不得,除非打点得很新巧,
　　　　否则由我看来还不如不用吧。

Lorenzo 'Tis now but four o'clock; we have two hours
To furnish us.

[Enter Launcelot, *With a letter.]*

Friend Launcelot, what's the news?

Launcelot An it shall please you to break up this, it shall
seem to signify.

Lorenzo I know the hand; in faith, 'tis a fair hand,
And whiter than the paper it writ on
Is the fair hand that writ.

Gratiano   Love news, in faith.

Launcelot By your leave, sir.

Lorenzo Whither goest thou?

Launcelot Marry, sir, to bid my old master, the Jew, to
sup to-night with my new master, the Christian.

Lorenzo Hold, here, take this. Tell gentle Jessica
I will not fail her; speak it privately.
Go, gentlemen,

[Exit Launcelot.]*

Will you prepare you for this masque to-night?
I am provided of a torch-bearer.

Salarino Ay, marry, I'll be gone about it straight.

Salanio And so will I.

Lorenzo   Meet me and Gratiano
At Gratiano's lodging some hour hence.

Salarino 'Tis good we do so.

[Exeunt Salarino *and* Salanio.]*

Gratiano Was not that letter from fair Jessica?

Lorenzo I must needs tell thee all. She hath directed
How I shall take her from her father's house;
What gold and jewels she is furnish'd with;
What page's suit she hath in readiness.
If e'er the Jew her father come to heaven,
It will be for his gentle daughter's sake;
And never dare misfortune cross her foot,
Unless she do it under this excuse,

洛　良　佐　　现在还只四点钟：我们有两小时
　　　　　　去准备。
　　　　　　　　　　　　［朗斯洛忒持信件上。
　　　　　　　　朗斯洛忒朋友，什么事？
朗 斯 洛 忒　若是您高兴把这打开来，它好似会告诉您。
洛　良　佐　我认得这笔迹：当真，这笔划真妙；
　　　　　　比这张洁白的信纸更要姣好的，
　　　　　　是那写字的凝脂美手。
葛拉希阿诺　　　　　　　　　　　　是情书。
朗 斯 洛 忒　大官人，小的告辞了。
洛　良　佐　你到哪儿去？
朗 斯 洛 忒　凭圣母，大官人，去请我的老主人那犹太人今晚上跟
　　　　　　我的新主人那基督徒一块儿吃饭。
洛　良　佐　且慢，这一点给你：你去回报
　　　　　　温婉的絮雪格，我不会误她的约；
　　　　　　悄悄地跟她说话。各位，去吧，　　　［朗斯洛忒下。
　　　　　　你们去准备今晚的假面跳舞吗？
　　　　　　我已经约好了一个执火把的僮儿。
萨 拉 里 诺　唔，凭圣母，我马上去准备起来。
萨 拉 尼 奥　我也去。
洛　良　佐　　　　　　再过点把钟，跟葛拉希阿诺
　　　　　　和我在他寓所里相会。
萨 拉 里 诺　这样很好。　　　　　　［萨拉里诺与萨拉尼奥同下。
葛拉希阿诺　那封信不是漂亮的絮雪格写的吗？
洛　良　佐　我定得把一切都告你。她关照了我
　　　　　　怎样将她从她父亲家接出来，
　　　　　　她将随身带什么样金珠宝贝，
　　　　　　她会预备好怎样的僮儿服装。
　　　　　　假如犹太佬她父亲能得升天，
　　　　　　那是因依仗他温婉的女儿之故。
　　　　　　逆运决不敢拦截她行进的步子，
　　　　　　只除了它可能采取那样的借口，

That she is issue to a faithless Jew.

Come, go with me, peruse this as thou goest;

Fair Jessica shall be my torch-bearer.

[*Exeunt.*]

SCENE V. The same. *Before* Shylock's *house*

[*Enter* Shylock *and* Launcelot.]

Shylock　Well, thou shalt see; thy eyes shall be thy
　　judge,

The difference of old Shylock and Bassanio: —

What, Jessica! — Thou shalt not gormandize,

As thou hast done with me; — What, Jessica! —

And sleep and snore, and rend apparel out—

Why, Jessica, I say!

Launcelot　　　　Why, Jessica!

Shylock　Who bids thee call? I do not bid thee call.

Launcelot　Your worship was wont to tell me I could do
　　nothing without bidding.

[*Enter* Jessica.]

Jessica　Call you? What is your will?

Shylock　I am bid forth to supper, Jessica:

There are my keys. But wherefore should I go?

I am not bid for love; they flatter me;

But yet I'll go in hate, to feed upon

The prodigal Christian. Jessica, my girl,

Look to my house. I am right loath to go;

There is some ill a-brewing towards my rest,

For I did dream of money-bags to-night.

Launcelot　I beseech you, sir, go: my young master doth
　　expect your reproach.

Shylock　So do I his.

Launcelot　And they have conspired together; I will
　　not say you shall see a masque, but if you do, then it

说因为奸邪的犹太人是她父亲。
来吧,和我一同去;边走边看信:
美好的絜雪格将是我执火把的佼童。

[同下。

第 五 景

[同前。夏洛克家门首]
[夏洛克与朗斯洛忒上。

夏 洛 克　好吧,你可以看到,你眼睛能判定,
老夏洛克跟跛萨尼奥的区别:——
什么,絜雪格! ——你再也不要穷吃了,
像你在我家一般:——什么,絜雪格! ——
还死睡,打鼾,把衣服胡乱撕烂;——
嗨,絜雪格,我说!

朗 斯 洛 忒　　　　　　　嗨,絜雪格!
夏 洛 克　谁要你叫的? 我没有要你叫啊。
朗 斯 洛 忒　您老人家老是告诉我,说不关照,我什么事也不
要干。

[絜雪格上。

絜 雪 格　您叫我吗? 有什么吩咐?
夏 洛 克　絜雪格,今儿我给请出去吃晚饭:
我的钥匙在这儿。但为何我要去?
我不是为爱而被邀;他们捧拍我:
可是我为了恨所以去,存心去吃吃
这个挥霍的基督徒。絜雪格吾女,
照看着门户。我很不乐意前去:
有什么不祥的兆头妨碍我安息,
因为我昨夜在梦里见到钱袋。

朗 斯 洛 忒　请您老人家务必去:我家少主人指望您斥责。
夏 洛 克　我也指望他斥责。
朗 斯 洛 忒　他们已经同谋好,我不说您会看到一场假面跳舞;可

was not for nothing that my nose fell a-bleeding on
Black Monday last at six o'clock i' the morning, fall-
ing out that year on Ash-Wednesday was four year in
the afternoon.

Shylock   What! are there masques? Hear you me, Jessica:
Lock up my doors, and when you hear the drum,
And the vile squealing of the wry-neck'd fife,
Clamber not you up to the casements then,
Nor thrust your head into the public street
To gaze on Christian fools with varnish'd faces;
But stop my house's ears- I mean my casements;
Let not the sound of shallow fopp'ry enter
My sober house. By Jacob's staff, I swear
I have no mind of feasting forth to-night;
But I will go. Go you before me, sirrah;
Say I will come.

Launcelot   I will go before, sir. Mistress, look out at
    window for all this;
    There will come a Christian by
    Will be worth a Jewess' eye.

                                                    [*Exit* Launcelot.]

Shylock   What says that fool of Hagar's offspring, ha?
Jessica   His words were *Farewell, mistress*; nothing else.
Shylock   The patch is kind enough, but a huge feeder;
Snail-slow in profit, and he sleeps by day
More than the wild-cat; drones hive not with me,
Therefore I part with him; and part with him
To one that I would have him help to waste
His borrow'd purse. Well, Jessica, go in;
Perhaps I will return immediately:
Do as I bid you, shut doors after you:
Fast bind, fast find,
A proverb never stale in thrifty mind.   [*Exit.*]
Jessica   Farewell; and if my fortune be not crost,
I have a father, you a daughter, lost.   [*Exit.*]

是您若看到的话,那就无怪上一个黑星期一早上六
点钟我的鼻子会流鼻血,那一年正是在圣灰节第四
年的下午。

夏　洛　克　什么,有假面跳舞? 听我说,絜雪格:
把门锁起来;当你听到击鼓声,
还有歪脖子的横笛那尖声怪叫,
可不准爬到窗棂上东张西望,
也不许伸出脑袋去探视街道,
瞧那些傻瓜基督徒油彩涂满脸;
要堵住这屋子的耳朵,我是说窗子:
别让那浮嚣蠢事的声音钻进我
这庄重的屋子。凭雅各的牧杖,
我今儿晚上真不想出外去赴宴:
可是还得去。你在头里走,小子;
说我就来到。

朗斯洛忒　我就先走了,您老。姑娘,不管这一切,探出窗外望。
　　　　　有个基督徒要来到,
　　　　　值得个犹太姑娘瞟。　　　　　　　　〔下。

夏　洛　克　那夏甲的傻瓜儿孙说些什么?

絜　雪　格　他说"再会了,姑娘";没有说别的。

夏　洛　克　这蠢货人倒还不坏,可肚子太大:
做事慢得像蜗牛,大白天睡觉
要赛过野猫;懒惰的雄蜂跟我
不相容;故而我送走他,把他送给那
举债度日的浪子,好帮他花费。
好了,絜雪格,进去:我也许马上
要回来:听我的,照办;关上了门户:
绑得牢,容易找;
这格言在勤俭人心上永不抛。　　　　　　〔下。

絜　雪　格　祝平安;若是我命运不遭挫折,
我有个父亲,您有个女儿,要丧失。
　　　　　　　　　　　　　　　　　　　　　〔下。

SCENE VI. *The same.*

[*Enter* Gratiano *and* Salarino, *masqued.*]

Gratiano This is the pent-house under which Lorenzo
Desir'd us to make stand.

Salarino   His hour is almost past.

Gratiano And it is marvel he out-dwells his hour,
For lovers ever run before the clock.

Salarino O! ten times faster Venus' pigeons fly
To seal love's bonds new made than they are wont
To keep obliged faith unforfeited!

Gratiano That ever holds: who riseth from a feast
With that keen appetite that he sits down?
Where is the horse that doth untread again
His tedious measures with the unbated fire
That he did pace them first? All things that are
Are with more spirit chased than enjoy'd.
How like a younker or a prodigal
The scarfed bark puts from her native bay,
Hugg'd and embraced by the strumpet wind!
How like the prodigal doth she return,
With over-weather'd ribs and ragged sails,
Lean, rent, and beggar'd by the strumpet wind!

Salarino Here comes Lorenzo; more of this hereafter.

[*Enter* Lorenzo.]

Lorenzo Sweet friends, your patience for my long abode;
Not I, but my affairs, have made you wait:
When you shall please to play the thieves for wives,
I'll watch as long for you then. Approach;

第 六 景

[同前]

[葛拉希阿诺与萨拉里诺戴假面上。

葛拉希阿诺 在这屋檐下,便是洛良佐要我们
来等他。

萨 拉 里 诺　　　　　他约定的时刻快要过了。

葛拉希阿诺 他会迟到真是件怪事,因为
恋爱的人们总赶在时钟前面。

萨 拉 里 诺 啊,维纳斯的瑞鸽飞去缔结
新欢的盟誓,总比使旧好能践行
要快上十倍!

葛拉希阿诺　　　　　　那是不易的常情:
谁从筵醮上宴罢起立时,还有他
当初刚入席那种饕餮的胃口?
哪有一匹马会用不减的精神
驰骋它疲劳的步蹄,如同开始
长驱时那样抖擞? 对人间事物,
追逐总要比享受更兴致勃勃。
多么像一个英俊活泼的青年,
那披着肩巾的快艇驶离了港口,
去受淫滥的风飚紧搂和拥抱!
或者像一个浪子,它回程返港,
龙肋给风吹雨打,篷帆残碎,
被淫雨消磨得羸瘦、破烂和潦倒!

萨 拉 里 诺 洛良佐来了:这些话以后再谈。

　　　　　　　　[洛良佐上。

洛 良 佐 两位好友,我来得太晚,请原谅;
因有事摆不脱身,累你们久等:
待你们将来也得偷妻子的时候,
我也会替你们守候这么久。上前来:

Here dwells my father Jew. Ho! who's within?

[*Enter* Jessica, *above, in boy's clothes.*]

Jessica   Who are you? Tell me, for more certainty,

Albeit I'll swear that I do know your tongue.

Lorenzo   Lorenzo, and thy love.

Jessica   Lorenzo, certain; and my love indeed,

For who love I so much? And now who knows

But you, Lorenzo, whether I am yours?

Lorenzo   Heaven and thy thoughts are witness that thou
art.

Jessica   Here, catch this casket; it is worth the pains.

I am glad 'tis night, you do not look on me,

For I am much asham'd of my exchange;

But love is blind, and lovers cannot see

The pretty follies that themselves commit,

For, if they could, Cupid himself would blush

To see me thus transformed to a boy.

Lorenzo   Descend, for you must be my torch-bearer.

Jessica   What! must I hold a candle to my shames?

They in themselves, good sooth, are too-too light.

Why, 'tis an office of discovery, love,

And I should be obscur'd.

Lorenzo   So are you, sweet,

Even in the lovely garnish of a boy.

But come at once;

For the close night doth play the runaway,

And we are stay'd for at Bassanio's feast.

Jessica   I will make fast the doors, and gild myself

With some moe ducats, and be with you straight.

[*Exit above.*]

Gratiano   Now, by my hood, a Gentile, and no Jew.

Lorenzo   Beshrew me, but I love her heartily;

　　　　　　　这是我犹太岳父家。嗨！里边谁？

　　　　　　　　［絜雪格着童子装在上方上。

絜　雪　格　你是什么人？告诉我，为了免差错，
　　　　　　　虽然我听得真切你那个声音。

洛　良　佐　我是洛良佐，你的心上人。

絜　雪　格　洛良佐，的确，果然是我的心上人，
　　　　　　　因为谁，我爱得这样亲切？除了你，
　　　　　　　洛良佐，谁知道我可是你的亲亲？

洛　良　佐　上天和你的思想证明你确是。

絜　雪　格　这里，接住这匣儿；它值得你费心。
　　　　　　　幸好这是在夜里，你瞧不见我，
　　　　　　　我装成这副模样，挺不好意思：
　　　　　　　可是恋爱是盲目的，着迷的恋人们
　　　　　　　瞧不见他们自己所干的傻事；
　　　　　　　因为假如他们能，邱璧特会脸红，
　　　　　　　当他看到我这样变化成僮儿。

洛　良　佐　下来，你得做我的火把执掌僮。

絜　雪　格　怎么，我得手拿着烛火，照亮我
　　　　　　　自己的羞惭吗？当真，它们已经
　　　　　　　太显耀，这件事可是在暴露，亲亲；
　　　　　　　我却应当受隐晦。

洛　良　佐　　　　　　　　　你就会，蜜蜜，
　　　　　　　穿上可爱的童装给隐蔽起来。
　　　　　　　可是，快来；
　　　　　　　这隐密的暗夜逃跑得好不飞快，
　　　　　　　而跋萨尼奥在等着我们去赴宴。

絜　雪　格　我来把门户关好，还要多装上
　　　　　　　几块金特格，然后立刻来就你。

　　　　　　　　　　　　　　　　　　　　　　［自上方下。

葛拉希阿诺　凭我的头巾打赌，她是个基督徒，
　　　　　　　不是个犹太人。

洛　良　佐　　　　　　　诅咒我，我若不爱她；

For she is wise, if I can judge of her,
And fair she is, if that mine eyes be true,
And true she is, as she hath prov'd herself;
And therefore, like herself, wise, fair, and true,
Shall she be placed in my constant soul.

[*Enter* Jessica.]

What, art thou come? On, gentlemen, away!
Our masquing mates by this time for us stay.

[*Exit with* Jessica *and* Salarino.]
[*Enter* Antonio.]

Antonio   Who's there?

Gratiano   Signior Antonio!

Antonio   Fie, fie, Gratiano! where are all the rest?
'Tis nine o'clock; our friends all stay for you.
No masque to-night: the wind is come about;
Bassanio presently will go aboard:
I have sent twenty out to seek for you.

Gratiano   I am glad on't: I desire no more delight
Than to be under sail and gone to-night.   [*Exeunt.*]

SCENE VII. Belmont. *A room in* Portia's *house.*

[*Flourish of cornets. Enter* Portia,
with the Prince of Morocco, *and their trains.*]

Portia   Go draw aside the curtains and discover
The several caskets to this noble prince.
Now make your choice.

Prince of Morocco   The first, of gold, who this inscrip-
tion bears:
Who chooseth me shall gain what many men desire.
The second, silver, which this promise carries:
Who chooseth me shall get as much as he deserves.
This third, dull lead, with warning all as blunt:
Who chooseth me must give and hazard all he hath.
How shall I know if I do choose the right?

我若是能判断，她真够聪明智慧，
我若是眼光真切，她真够美艳，
而她已经证明了，她又加是真诚，
像这样聪慧、美丽、真诚的女子，
她将在我恒久的灵魂里永保存。

〔絜雪格在下方上。

啊，你来了？行进，朋友们；去来！
我们的舞伴正在把我们等待。

〔与絜雪格、萨拉里诺同下。

〔安东尼奥上。

安东尼奥 那边是谁？

葛拉希阿诺 安东尼奥舍人！

安东尼奥 得了，得了，葛拉希阿诺！大伙呢？
已经九点钟：朋友们都等着你们。
今晚没有假面舞：顺风已来到；
跋萨尼奥就要立刻上船去：
我差了二十个人来寻找你们。

葛拉希阿诺 我好不高兴：我一心只是急巴巴，
盼望今晚上就能扬帆出发。 〔同下。

第 七 景

〔贝尔蒙。宝喜霞邸内一室〕
〔长鸣齐奏。宝喜霞及摩洛哥亲王，各率随从上。

宝 喜 霞 去拽开帷幕，把几只匣儿显露给
这位尊贵的亲王。现在请您挑。

摩 洛 哥 第一只是金的，刻着这样的题辞，
"谁挑选了我，会得到众人之所愿"；
第二只是银的，附着这样的规约，
"谁挑选了我，会得到他的所应有"；
第三只，纯铅铸，附着的警告也突兀，
"谁挑选了我，得牺牲、冒险他的一切。"
我怎能知道我挑的正巧对劲？

Portia   The one of them contains my picture, prince;
If you choose that, then I am yours withal.
Prince of Morocco   Some god direct my judgment! Let me
  see;
I will survey the inscriptions back again.
What says this leaden casket?
Who chooseth me must give and hazard all he hath.
Must give; for what? For lead? Hazard for lead!
This casket threatens; men that hazard all
Do it in hope of fair advantages;
A golden mind stoops not to shows of dross;
I'll then nor give nor hazard aught for lead.
What says the silver with her virgin hue?
Who chooseth me shall get as much as he deserves.
As much as he deserves! Pause there, Morocco,
And weigh thy value with an even hand.
If thou be'st rated by thy estimation,
Thou dost deserve enough, and yet enough
May not extend so far as to the lady;
And yet to be afeard of my deserving
Were but a weak disabling of myself.
As much as I deserve! Why, that's the lady;
I do in birth deserve her, and in fortunes,
In graces, and in qualities of breeding;
But more than these, in love I do deserve.
What if I stray'd no farther, but chose here?
Let's see once more this saying grav'd in gold;
Who chooseth me shall gain what many men desire.
Why, that's the lady; all the world desires her;
From the four corners of the earth they come,
To kiss this shrine, this mortal-breathing saint;
The Hyrcanian deserts and the vasty wilds
Of wide Arabia are as throughfares now
For princes to come view fair Portia;

宝　喜　霞　它们中有一只有我的图像,亲王;
　　　　　　您若是挑中它,我就归您所有。

摩　洛　哥　望天神指引我的判断! 容我想一下;
　　　　　　我回头从新来审查这几句铭辞。
　　　　　　这铅匣怎么说?
　　　　　　"谁挑选了我,得牺牲、冒险他的一切。"
　　　　　　得牺牲:为什么? 为铅? 为铅而冒险?
　　　　　　这匣儿威胁人。孤注一掷的人们,
　　　　　　那么干只为了能赢得优惠的好处;
　　　　　　一个金贵人不为了渣滓去弯腰;
　　　　　　我那就不为钝铅去牺牲或冒险。
　　　　　　白银怎么说,闪着它清贞的色泽?
　　　　　　"谁挑选了我,会得到他的所应有"。
　　　　　　得到我的所应有! 且稍待,摩洛哥,
　　　　　　用平稳的手法权衡你真正的价值,
　　　　　　若是你被评价时,你自己去估量,
　　　　　　你是否应得足够多;可是足够多,
　　　　　　并不意味着应得这姑娘千金秀,
　　　　　　不过为我的所应有平白地担忧,
　　　　　　只是无端损伤我自己的资格。
　　　　　　我的所应有! 哦,那就是这姑娘;
　　　　　　我在家世上应有她,财产配得过,
　　　　　　品性比得上,教养也十分相当;
　　　　　　但超越这一切,我在爱情上应有她。
　　　　　　是否我不再犹豫,就在此选定?
　　　　　　容我再一次瞧这金匣上的刻字;
　　　　　　"谁挑选了我会得到众人之所愿"。
　　　　　　哦,那正是这姑娘;全世界都但愿
　　　　　　得到她;他们从四面八方齐来到,
　　　　　　来吻敬这神灵,这呼吸的人间灵圣;
　　　　　　候坎尼亚的沙漠和广大的阿剌伯
　　　　　　辽阔荒野,已变成王子贵胄们
　　　　　　来瞻仰美貌的宝喜霞的通衢大道;

The watery kingdom, whose ambitious head
Spits in the face of heaven, is no bar
To stop the foreign spirits, but they come
As o'er a brook to see fair Portia.
One of these three contains her heavenly picture.
Is't like that lead contains her? 'Twere damnation
To think so base a thought; it were too gross
To rib her cerecloth in the obscure grave.
Or shall I think in silver she's immur'd,
Being ten times undervalu'd to tried gold?
O sinful thought! Never so rich a gem
Was set in worse than gold. They have in England
A coin that bears the figure of an angel
Stamped in gold; but that's insculp'd upon;
But here an angel in a golden bed
Lies all within. Deliver me the key;
Here do I choose, and thrive I as I may!

Portia   There, take it, prince, and if my form lie there,
Then I am yours.

[*He unlocks the golden casket.*]

Prince of Morocco   O hell! what have we here?
A carrion Death, within whose empty eye
There is a written scroll! I'll read the writing.

All that glisters is not gold,
Often have you heard that told;
Many a man his life hath sold
But my outside to behold:
Gilded tombs do worms infold.
Had you been as wise as bold,
Young in limbs, in judgment old,
Your answer had not been inscroll'd:
Fare you well, your suit is cold.

汹涌澎湃的王邦，它雄心勃勃，抬头
吐唾沫泼天颜，也不能阻止纷纷
从外国联翩汇集的远客，他们来，
像跨过一条小河，访绝色的宝喜霞。
这三中之一有她天仙似的肖像。
是否铅匣里有他？这卑劣的想法
简直是亵渎：即令是她裹尸的蜡布，
放在这黝暗的墓里也太荒谬。
我应否设想她幽闭在银匣里边？
——白银比久经试验的黄金贱十倍；
啊，罪辜的想法！这样的琼琚，
决不能不用精金镶。他们在英格兰
有一种钱币印着个天使的形象，
是黄金所铸，但那是镌刻而成的，
而这里这天使是在黄金床上，
躺在匣中央。给我一柄钥匙；
我挑定这匣儿，但愿我吉运昌隆！

宝　喜　霞　这里，接着，亲王；我的像若在此，
我便是您的。　　　　　　　　　　　[他开启金匣。

摩　洛　哥　　　　　暖呀！这是什么啊？
一个死尸的骷髅，在它眼眶里
有一个写字的纸卷！我来念一下。
[读]闪闪发光的不都是黄金；
　　素常的说法总这样声称：
　　世上好多人毁掉了一生，
　　只为了能看到我的外形：
　　蛆虫占据着镀金的墓茔，
　　你要是既勇敢而又聪明，
　　判断已老成，手脚虽轻灵，
　　答复便不会叫你去伤心：
　　祝平安；你求到一片寒冰。

Cold indeed; and labour lost:
Then, farewell, heat, and welcome, frost!
Portia, adieu! I have too griev'd a heart
To take a tedious leave; thus losers part.

     [*Exit with his train. Flourish of cornets.*]

Portia A gentle riddance. Draw the curtains: go.
Let all of his complexion choose me so.

            [*Exeunt.*]

SCENE VIII. Venice. *A street*

     [*Enter* Salarino *and* Salanio.]

Salarino Why, man, I saw Bassanio under sail;
With him is Gratiano gone along;
And in their ship I am sure Lorenzo is not.

Salanio The villain Jew with outcries rais'd the Duke,
Who went with him to search Bassanio's ship.

Salarino He came too late, the ship was under sail;
But there the duke was given to understand
That in a gondola were seen together
Lorenzo and his amorous Jessica.
Besides, Antonio certified the duke
They were not with Bassanio in his ship.

Salanio I never heard a passion so confus'd,
So strange, outrageous, and so variable,
As the dog Jew did utter in the streets.
My daughter! O my ducats! O my daughter!
Fled with a Christian! O my Christian ducats!
Justice! the law! my ducats and my daughter!
A sealed bag, two sealed bags of ducats,
Of double ducats, stol'n from me by my daughter!

一片寒冰，果真是；枉费了心机：
那么，作别了，热情！冰霜啊，良契！
宝喜霞，祝平安。我太失意而悲伤，
不能够依依道别：孤注者输光。

               [率扈从下。长鸣齐奏。

宝 喜 霞 厄运去得还轻快。拽上了帷幕。
愿像他这样容貌的都这般挑我。

               [同下。

第 八 景

[威尼斯。一街道]
[萨拉里诺与萨拉尼奥上。

萨拉里诺 是啊，老兄，我眼见跋萨尼奥走：
跟他一起的只有葛拉希阿诺；
我分明不见洛良佐在他们船上。

萨拉尼奥 那犹太坏蛋呼号着惊动了公爵，
他只得同他去搜查待开的船了。

萨拉里诺 他来得太晚，船已经扬帆开出：
可是公爵在那儿被明白告知，
有人见到在一只平底艑舻里，
洛良佐同他多情的絮雪格在夜游：
安东尼奥又复向公爵作保证，
他们并不在跋萨尼奥的船上。

萨拉尼奥 我从未听到过这样混乱的哀号，
那么样怪异、暴戾，那么样多变化，
如那条犹太疯狗在街上所嚷的，
"我女儿！啊呀，我的金特格！女儿啊！
跟个基督徒逃跑了！基督特格啊！
公道啊！法律！金特格！啊也，我女儿！
一袋封好的，两袋封好的特格，
双特格，唉呀，给我女儿偷走啊！

And jewels! two stones, two rich and precious stones,
Stol'n by my daughter! Justice! find the girl!
She hath the stones upon her and the ducats.

Salarino Why, all the boys in Venice follow him,
Crying, *his stones, his daughter,* and *his ducats.*

Salanio Let good Antonio look he keep his day,
Or he shall pay for this.

Salarino   Marry, well remember'd.
I reason'd with a Frenchman yesterday,
Who told me, — in the narrow seas that part
The French and English, — there miscarried
A vessel of our country richly fraught.
I thought upon Antonio when he told me,
And wish'd in silence that it were not his.

Salanio You were best to tell Antonio what you hear;
Yet do not suddenly, for it may grieve him.

Salarino A kinder gentleman treads not the earth.
I saw Bassanio and Antonio part:
Bassanio told him he would make some speed
Of his return. He answer'd Do not so;
Slubber not business for my sake, Bassanio,
But stay the very riping of the time;
And for the Jew's bond which he hath of me,
Let it not enter in your mind of love:
Be merry, and employ your chiefest thoughts
To courtship, and such fair ostents of love
As shall conveniently become you there.
And even there, his eye being big with tears,
Turning his face, he put his hand behind him,
And with affection wondrous sensible
He wrung Bassanio's hand; and so they parted.

Salanio I think he only loves the world for him.

　　　　　　　　还有宝石，两大颗，珍贵的宝石呀，
　　　　　　　　给我女儿偷走啊！公道啊！找到她；
　　　　　　　　她身上藏着宝石哪，还有金特格。"

萨 拉 里 诺　可不是，威尼斯所有的孩子跟着他，
　　　　　　　　叫喊着，他的宝石、女儿啊、金特格。

萨 拉 尼 奥　安东尼奥得记住别误了期限，不然
　　　　　　　　他会付出代价。

萨 拉 里 诺　　　　　　　　凭玛丽，记得对。
　　　　　　　　昨天我跟个法兰西人闲谈，
　　　　　　　　他告我在那分隔开他们英法
　　　　　　　　两邦的狭海上，有一艘我们的船
　　　　　　　　满载着，失事了：他说时我就想到
　　　　　　　　安东尼奥；我心中默愿那不是
　　　　　　　　他的船。

萨 拉 尼 奥　　　　　你最好告诉了安东尼奥；
　　　　　　　　可不要太突然，免得他着急。

萨 拉 里 诺　这世上没有个仁霭超过他的士君子。
　　　　　　　　我瞧见他跟跋萨尼奥相离别：
　　　　　　　　跋萨尼奥告诉他说要早一点
　　　　　　　　回来：他答道，"别那样，跋萨尼奥，
　　　　　　　　不用为我的缘故疏误了正事，
　　　　　　　　却要功成事就后从容地回来；
　　　　　　　　至于我签给犹太人的债券合约，
　　　　　　　　别让它挂在你对我爱顾的心上：
　　　　　　　　要一团高兴，把你整个儿心思
　　　　　　　　放在求婚和优美的钟情神态上，
　　　　　　　　总要跟你在那里的身份相称。"
　　　　　　　　正在那当儿，他眼中噙满了眼泪，
　　　　　　　　将头背过去，他把手伸到后面，
　　　　　　　　以无比衷心感念的温情紧握着
　　　　　　　　跋萨尼奥；他们便这样相道别。

萨 拉 尼 奥　我想他爱这世界只是为了他，

I pray thee, let us go and find him out,
And quicken his embraced heaviness
With some delight or other.
Salarino   Do we so.   [*Exeunt.*]

SCENE IX. Belmont. *A room in* Portia's *house.*

[*Enter* Nerissa, *with a* Servitor.]

Nerissa   Quick, quick, I pray thee, draw the curtain
        straight;
The Prince of Arragon hath ta'en his oath,
And comes to his election presently.

[*Flourish of cornets. Enter the Prince* of Arragon,
            Portia, *and their Trains.*]

Portia   Behold, there stand the caskets, noble Prince:
If you choose that wherein I am contain'd,
Straight shall our nuptial rites be solemniz'd;
But if you fail, without more speech, my lord,
You must be gone from hence immediately.

Arragon   I am enjoin'd by oath to observe three things:
First, never to unfold to any one
Which casket 'twas I chose; next, if I fail
Of the right casket, never in my life
To woo a maid in way of marriage;
Lastly, if I do fail in fortune of my choice,
Immediately to leave you and be gone.

Portia   To these injunctions every one doth swear
That comes to hazard for my worthless self.

Arragon   And so have I address'd me. Fortune now
To my heart's hope! Gold, silver, and base lead.
Who chooseth me must give and hazard all he hath.
You shall look fairer ere I give or hazard.
What says the golden chest? Ha! let me see:

我说,我们务必要前去找到他,
用不拘什么欢心事,解开他心头
郁紧的愁闷。

萨 拉 里 诺 我们就去这么办。

[同下。

第 九 景

[贝尔蒙。宝喜霞邸内一室]
[纳丽莎与一仆从上。

纳 丽 莎 赶快,赶快,请务必;拽开这帷幕;
阿拉贡亲王已经宣过了信誓,
马上要到这里来作他的挑选。

　　　[长鸣齐奏。阿拉贡亲王,及宝喜霞,各率随从上。

宝 喜 霞 您瞧,尊贵的亲王,匣儿就在此:
要是您挑选正中了有我的那只,
我们的婚礼立刻就可以举行:
但假使您失败,殿下,不用再多讲,
您就得马上离这里别处去。

阿 拉 贡 我经过宣誓必须遵守三桩事:
首先,决不可告诉任何人我选了
哪一只匣儿,其次,假如挑不准
那对的匣儿,我从此终身决不向
任何女子去求婚:最后,我如果
挑选不走运,立即离您往别处。

宝 喜 霞 对这些训令,每一位曾来为我
这微贱的身躯冒险的,都宣过了誓。

阿 拉 贡 我已经准备就绪。但愿命运
满足我的愿望! 金匣,银匣,贱铅匣。
"谁挑选了我,得牺牲、冒险他的一切"。
我牺牲或冒险之前,你得美观些。
金匣儿怎么样说法? 嚇! 我来瞧;

Who chooseth me shall gain what many men desire.
What many men desire! that many may be meant
By the fool multitude, that choose by show,
Not learning more than the fond eye doth teach;
Which pries not to th' interior, but, like the martlet,
Builds in the weather on the outward wall,
Even in the force and road of casualty.
I will not choose what many men desire,
Because I will not jump with common spirits
And rank me with the barbarous multitudes.
Why, then to thee, thou silver treasure-house;
Tell me once more what title thou dost bear:
Who chooseth me shall get as much as he deserves.
And well said too; for who shall go about
To cozen fortune, and be honourable
Without the stamp of merit? Let none presume
To wear an undeserved dignity.
O! that estates, degrees, and offices
Were not deriv'd corruptly, and that clear honour
Were purchas'd by the merit of the wearer!
How many then should cover that stand bare;
How many be commanded that command;
How much low peasantry would then be glean'd
From the true seed of honour; and how much honour
Pick'd from the chaff and ruin of the times
To be new varnish'd! Well, but to my choice:
Who chooseth me shall get as much as he deserves.
I will assume desert. Give me a key for this,
And instantly unlock my fortunes here.

[*He opens the silver casket.*]

Portia   Too long a pause for that which you find there.
Arragon   What's here? The portrait of a blinking idiot,

"谁挑选了我会得到众人之所愿"。
众人之所愿！那众人也许是指
愚蠢的大众，他们凭外表挑选，
不想多懂些，超脱愚昧的眼光；
不知去窥察到里边，但像那紫燕，
不顾风吹雨打，在外墙上营巢，
时刻凌冒着不虞的变故灾祸。
我不去挑选那个众人之所愿，
因为我不愿跟随俗子共浮沉，
厕身在蛮野无文的庸众之间。
啊，那么，就你吧，白银的宝库；
再一次告诉我你佩着什么标题：
"谁挑选了我会得到他的所应有"；
说得多得体；因为谁会去行走，
为诳骗命运而依然得到尊荣，
若没有优良的品德？莫让任何人
胆敢凭空装一副不该有的庄严。
啊，但愿得财产、等第和权位
不是靠腐败钻营来，清白的光荣
只由享有者的优良品德所获致！
多少人在此脱帽站着的应加冠！
多少人发着号令的应当去听命！
多少名低微的鄙夫会从真正
光荣的种子中被搜检出来！多少位
光荣的俊彦从时俗的糠秕里选拔
出来，新加上光彩！好吧，我来挑：
"谁挑选了我会得到他的所应有"。
我要自认为应有。给我柄钥匙，
立即开启我在这匣儿里的命运。

〔开银匣。

宝 喜 霞　为您在那里边见到的待得太久了。
阿 拉 贡　是什么？一个闪眼傻瓜的画像，

Presenting me a schedule! I will read it.

How much unlike art thou to Portia!

How much unlike my hopes and my deservings!

Who chooseth me shall have as much as he deserves.

Did I deserve no more than a fool's head?

Is that my prize? Are my deserts no better?

Portia   To offend, and judge, are distinct offices,

And of opposed natures.

Arragon   What is here?

[*Reads.*] *The fire seven times tried this;*

        Seven times tried that judgment is

        That did never choose amiss.

        Some there be that shadows kiss;

        Such have but a shadow's bliss;

        There be fools alive, I wis,

        Silver'd o'er, and so was this.

        Take what wife you will to bed,

        I will ever be your head:

        So be gone; you are sped.

Still more fool I shall appear

By the time I linger here;

With one fool's head I came to woo,

But I go away with two.

Sweet, adieu! I'll keep my oath,

Patiently to bear my wroth.

                [*Exit* Aragon *with his train.*]

Portia   Thus hath the candle sing'd the moth.

O, these deliberate fools! When they do choose,

They have the wisdom by their wit to lose.

Nerissa   The ancient saying is no heresy:

Hanging and wiving goes by destiny.

Portia   Come, draw the curtain, Nerissa.

　　　　　　给我一张字条! 待我来念念。
　　　　　　你多么丝毫不跟宝喜霞相像!
　　　　　　多么跟我所应有的希望相像!
　　　　　　"谁挑选了我会得到他的所应有"。
　　　　　　我难道只应有一个傻瓜的头吗?
　　　　　　这是我的彩头吗? 我只应有这个?

宝　喜　霞　犯错误和评判是全然不同的两码事,
　　　　　　而且性质正相反。

阿　拉　贡　　　　　　　　　写的是什么?
　　　　　　[念]烈火锻炼过这银子七遍:
　　　　　　　　那个从不判断错的预见,
　　　　　　　　也定必经过七次的考验。
　　　　　　　　世上有些人把虚枉当真诠,
　　　　　　　　捉到个影子,只浮光一现。
　　　　　　　　我知道有些傻瓜在人间,
　　　　　　　　银装耀眼,如这个在眼前。
　　　　　　　　不管你娶个怎样的老婆,
　　　　　　　　我总是注定了是你的头颅。
　　　　　　　　故而,就去吧:快走,莫噜哕。
　　　　　　我要是再待在这儿发呆,
　　　　　　就越发显得是一个蠢才;
　　　　　　我带来一个傻脑袋求婚,
　　　　　　去时顶一对蠢头颅登程。
　　　　　　别了,美姣娘。我遵守誓言,
　　　　　　耐心去挨受愤怒的熬煎。

　　　　　　　　　　　　　　　　[阿拉贡亲王率扈从下。

宝　喜　霞　蜡烛便这般使扑火飞蛾遭了焚。
　　　　　　哎呀,这些蓄意的傻虫! 当他们
　　　　　　挑选时,都不中,只因太聪明,误前程。

纳　丽　莎　古话说得对,不是邪言和左道,
　　　　　　绞首和娶妻得仗命运来关照。

宝　喜　霞　来吧,拽好了帷幕,纳丽莎。

[*Enter a Servant.*]

Servant   Where is my lady?

Portia   Here; what would my lord?

Servant   Madam, there is alighted at your gate

A young Venetian, one that comes before

To signify th' approaching of his lord;

From whom he bringeth sensible regrets;

To wit, — besides commends and courteous breath, —

Gifts of rich value. Yet I have not seen

So likely an ambassador of love.

A day in April never came so sweet,

To show how costly summer was at hand,

As this fore-spurrer comes before his lord.

Portia   No more, I pray thee; I am half afeard

Thou wilt say anon he is some kin to thee,

Thou spend'st such high-day wit in praising him.

Come, come, Nerissa, for I long to see

Quick Cupid's post that comes so mannerly.

Nerissa   Bassanio, lord Love, if thy will it be!

[*Exeunt.*]

[一仆人上。

仆　　人　姑娘在哪儿?

宝　喜　霞　　　　　这儿:阁下怎么啦?

仆　　人　姑娘,在您府门口下马了一位
　　　　　年轻的威尼斯人,他被先遣来
　　　　　报道他少主不久即将来到;
　　　　　他带着他主人对您的殷勤致意,
　　　　　就是说,除了赏赞和谦恭的言语外,
　　　　　有珍贵的礼品。我从来没见过
　　　　　这样一位得体的钟情的使臣:
　　　　　一个四月天的日子从不如此媚,
　　　　　来预报华美的盛夏快要来贲临,
　　　　　如这位先驱比他主人赶先到。

宝　喜　霞　别再这么往下说了:我倒有点怕
　　　　　你接着就会说他是你自己的亲戚,
　　　　　你挥洒如许华言隽语来夸他。
　　　　　来吧,来吧,纳丽莎;我很想瞧瞧
　　　　　邱璧特的捷足使者风光这么俏。

纳　丽　莎　爱神啊,但愿来的是跋萨尼奥!

　　　　　　　　　　　　　　　　　　[同下。

ACT III.

SCENE I. Venice. *A street*

[*Enter* Salanio *and* Salarino.]

Salanio   Now, what news on the Rialto?

Salarino   Why, yet it lives there unchecked that Antonio hath a ship of rich lading wrack'd on the narrow seas; the Goodwins, I think they call the place, a very dangerous flat and fatal, where the carcasses of many a tall ship lie buried, as they say, if my gossip Report be an honest woman of her word.

Salanio   I would she were as lying a gossip in that as ever knapped ginger or made her neighbours believe she wept for the death of a third husband. But it is true, — without any slips of prolixity or crossing the plain highway of talk, — that the good Antonio, the honest Antonio, — O that I had a title good enough to keep his name company! —

Salarino   Come, the full stop.

Salanio   Ha! What sayest thou? Why, the end is, he hath lost a ship.

Salarino   I would it might prove the end of his losses.

Salanio   Let me say *amen* betimes, lest the devil cross my prayer, for here he comes in the likeness of a Jew.

[*Enter* Shylock.]

How now, Shylock! What news among the merchants?

第 三 幕

第 一 景

[威尼斯。一街道]
[萨拉尼奥与萨拉里纳上。

萨 拉 尼 奥　却说,市场里有什么消息?

萨 拉 里 诺　是啊,那里这传闻没有否定,说安东尼奥有一条满载
的船在海峡里沉没了;他们管那地方叫古特温;是一
处很危险的致命的浅滩,那儿好多艘巨舟的尸骸埋
葬着,他们说,假使传闻是可靠的话。

萨 拉 尼 奥　我但愿那传闻像一个喈喈糖姜、要她街坊们相信她
为她第三个丈夫死去而哭泣的婆娘一样靠不住。可
是那是真实的说法,没有罗嗦累赘的过误或要言不
明的疏失,这位好安东尼奥,老实的安东尼奥——
啊,但 愿 我 有 个 够 好 的 徽 号 来 加 在 他 名 字
前面!——

萨 拉 里 诺　说呀,话没有说完。

萨 拉 尼 奥　嘛!你说什么?唉,总的说来,他丢了一条船。

萨 拉 里 诺　但愿这是他末了一次损失。

萨 拉 尼 奥　让我及时叫"亚门",否则魔鬼要掐断我的祷告,因为
他装成一个犹太人的模样到来了。

[夏洛克上。

怎么说,哎,夏洛克!商人中间有什么消息?

Shylock You knew, none so well, none so well as you, of my daughter's flight.

Salarino That's certain; I, for my part, knew the tailor that made the wings she flew withal.

Salanio And Shylock, for his own part, knew the bird was fledged; and then it is the complexion of them all to leave the dam.

Shylock She is damned for it.

Salarino That's certain, if the devil may be her judge.

Shylock My own flesh and blood to rebel!

Salanio Out upon it, old carrion! Rebels it at these years?

Shylock I say my daughter is my flesh and my blood.

Salarino There is more difference between thy flesh and hers than between jet and ivory; more between your bloods than there is between red wine and Rhenish. But tell us, do you hear whether Antonio have had any loss at sea or no?

Shylock There I have another bad match: a bankrupt, a prodigal, who dare scarce show his head on the Rialto; a beggar, that used to come so smug upon the mart; let him look to his bond: he was wont to call me usurer; let him look to his bond: he was wont to lend money for a Christian courtesy; let him look to his bond.

Salarino Why, I am sure, if he forfeit, thou wilt not take his flesh: what's that good for?

Shylock To bait fish withal: if it will feed nothing else, it will feed my revenge. He hath disgrac'd me and hind'red me half a million; laugh'd at my losses, mock'd at my gains, scorned my nation, thwarted my bargains, cooled my friends, heated mine enemies. And what's his reason? I am a Jew. Hath not a Jew eyes? Hath not a Jew hands, organs, dimensions, senses, affections, passions, fed with the same food, hurt with the same weapons, subject to the same diseases, healed by the same means, warmed and cooled by the same winter and summer, as a Christian is? If you prick us, do we not bleed? If you tickle us, do

夏　洛　克　你们知道,没有谁这么清楚,跟你们一样清楚,我女儿逃跑了。

萨拉里诺　那当然啰:我,拿我来说,便知道替她缝制她飞走的翅膀的那个裁缝。

萨拉尼奥　而夏洛克,对他来说,也知道她已经长好了羽毛;她们的态势是都要离开娘亲的。

夏　洛　克　为此她得下地狱。

萨拉里诺　那是必定的,假如魔鬼做她的判官。

夏　洛　克　我亲生的血肉反叛我!

萨拉尼奥　去它的,烂肉! 这么大年纪还反叛?

夏　洛　克　我是说我女儿是我的血肉。

萨拉里诺　你的血跟她的,差别比黑肉和象牙还大;你们的血比普通的红酒和莱因河名酒相差还大。可是,告诉我们,你听到过安东尼奥在海上有没有损失?

夏　洛　克　那是我又一桩倒霉事:一个破产家伙,一个浪荡子,他不敢在市场上露脸了;一个花子,素常到市场上来总穿戴得衣冠齐楚:让他注意那借据立约:他惯常骂我重利盘剥;让他注意那借据立约:他惯常放债凭基督徒的情意不收息金;让他注意那借据立约。

萨拉里诺　我说,要是他失约,我相信你不会要他的肉;那有什么用处?

夏　洛　克　作钓鱼用:假使不能喂别的,可以满足我的仇恨。他污辱了我,叫我吃亏五十万;耻笑我的损失,讥刺我的赢利,侮蔑我的种族,破坏我的买卖契约,泼我的朋友们冷水,搧我的仇家的火势;他可有什么道理?我是个犹太人。犹太人没有眼睛吗? 犹太人没有手脚、器官、身材大小、感觉、情意、血性吗? 跟一个基督徒不是吃同样的食品,用同样的刀枪可以伤害他,也同样会害病,用同样的药剂可以医治,同样的冬天和夏天可以使他冷和热吗? 你若戳刺我们,我们不会出血吗? 你若逗我们痒,我们不会笑吗? 你若用

we not laugh? If you poison us, do we not die? And if you wrong us, shall we not revenge? If we are like you in the rest, we will resemble you in that. If a Jew wrong a Christian, what is his humility? Revenge. If a Christian wrong a Jew, what should his sufferance be by Christian example? Why, revenge. The villainy you teach me I will execute; and it shall go hard but I will better the instruction.

[*Enter a* Servant.]

Servant Gentlemen, my master Antonio is at his house, and desires to speak with you both.

Salarino We have been up and down to seek him.

[*Enter* Tubal.]

Salanio Here comes another of the tribe; a third cannot be match'd, unless the devil himself turn Jew.

[*Exeunt* Salanio, Salarino, *and* Servant.]

Shylock How now, Tubal! what news from Genoa? Hast thou found my daughter?

Tubal I often came where I did hear of her, but cannot find her.

Shylock Why there, there, there, there! A diamond gone, cost me two thousand ducats in Frankfort! The curse never fell upon our nation till now; I never felt it till now. Two thousand ducats in that, and other precious, precious jewels. I would my daughter were dead at my foot, and the jewels in her ear; would she were hearsed at my foot, and the ducats in her coffin! No news of them? Why, so: and I know not what's spent in the search. Why, thou—loss upon loss! The thief gone with so much, and so much to find the thief; and no satisfaction, no revenge; nor no ill luck stirring but what lights on my shoulders; no sighs but of my breathing; no tears but of my shedding.

Tubal Yes, other men have ill luck too. Antonio, as I heard in Genoa, —

毒药毒我们,我们不会死吗?而你若伤害我们,我们
能不报复吗?要是我们在其他事情上跟你们一样,
我们在某一件事上也跟你们相同。要是一个犹太人
伤害了一个基督徒,那基督徒怎样表示他的谦让?
报复。要是一个基督徒伤害了一个犹太人,根据基
督徒的榜样,那个犹太人应当怎样表示他的宽容?
报复,当然。你教给我的恶辣手段,我要来实行,并
且要从严回敬。

　　　　　〔一仆人上。

仆　　　人　官人们,我主人安东尼奥在家,想请两位去谈话。

萨 拉 里 诺　我们正在到处找他呢。

　　　　　〔屠勃尔上。

萨 拉 尼 奥　他那种族里又来了一个:第三个再也找不到,除非魔
　　　　　鬼自己变成了犹太人。

　　　　　　　　　〔萨拉尼奥、萨拉里诺与仆人下。

夏　洛　克　怎么说,屠勃尔?热内亚有什么消息来?你找到了
　　　　　我女儿吗?

屠　勃　尔　我老是在她到过的地方听到人家说起她,可找不
　　　　　到她。

夏　洛　克　唉,该死,该死,该死,该死!一颗钻石完了,我在法
　　　　　兰克福花了两千金特格买进的!直到现在诅咒才落
　　　　　到我们民族头上;现在我真正感觉到了:那里头有两
　　　　　千金特格;还有别的珍宝啊,珍宝。我但愿我女儿在
　　　　　我脚旁边死了,而那些宝石挂在她耳上!但愿她在
　　　　　我脚旁的棺材里,而那些金特格在她棺中!没有他
　　　　　们的消息吗?唉,就这样:我不知道为寻找他们,又
　　　　　花了多少;唉,你这损失上再加损失!贼偷了这么多
　　　　　走了,又花了这么多去找那个贼;可没有得到满足,
　　　　　得到报复;没有恶运气不是降在我这肩上的;只有我
　　　　　在悲叹,只有我在哭泣。

屠　勃　尔　不,别人也有倒霉的:安东尼奥,我在热那亚听
　　　　　说,——

Shylock What, what, what? Ill luck, ill luck?

Tubal hath an argosy cast away, coming from Tripolis.

Shylock I thank God! I thank God! Is it true, is it true?

Tubal I spoke with some of the sailors that escaped the wrack.

Shylock I thank thee, good Tubal. Good news, good news! ha, ha! Where? in Genoa?

Tubal Your daughter spent in Genoa, as I heard, one night, fourscore ducats.

Shylock Thou stick'st a dagger in me: I shall never see my gold again: fourscore ducats at a sitting! Fourscore ducats!

Tubal There came divers of Antonio's creditors in my company to Venice that swear he cannot choose but break.

Shylock I am very glad of it; I'll plague him, I'll torture him; I am glad of it.

Tubal One of them showed me a ring that he had of your daughter for a monkey.

Shylock Out upon her! Thou torturest me, Tubal: It was my turquoise; I had it of Leah when I was a bachelor; I would not have given it for a wilderness of monkeys.

Tubal But Antonio is certainly undone.

Shylock Nay, that's true; that's very true. Go, Tubal, fee me an officer; bespeak him a fortnight before. I will have the heart of him, if he forfeit; for, were he out of Venice, I can make what merchandise I will. Go, Tubal, and meet me at our synagogue; go, good Tubal; at our synagogue, Tubal.   [*Exeunt.*]

SCENE II. Belmont. *A room in* Portia's *house.*

[*Enter* Bassanio, Portia, Gratiano, Nerissa, *and* Attendants.]

Portia I pray you tarry; pause a day or two
Before you hazard; for, in choosing wrong,

夏　洛　克　什么,什么,什么? 倒霉,倒霉?

屠　勃　尔　有一艘海舶丢掉了,从屈黎波里来。

夏　洛　克　多谢上帝,多谢上帝。真的吗,真的吗?

屠　勃　尔　我跟几个逃过触礁的水手讲过话。

夏　洛　克　多谢你,好屠勃尔:好消息,好消息! 哈哈! 在哪里? 在热那亚?

屠　勃　尔　我听说,你女儿在热那亚一夜花掉八十块金特格。

夏　洛　克　你戳了我一刀:我再也见不到我的金元了:一下子就丢掉八十块! 八十块金特格。

屠　勃　尔　有安东尼奥的几个债主同我一起到威尼斯,他们赌咒他非破产不行。

夏　洛　克　我高兴得不得了:我要折磨他;我要毒害他:我好不高兴。

屠　勃　尔　他们之中有一个给我看一只指环,是他用一只猴子向你女儿换来的。

夏　洛　克　去她的! 你毒害我,屠勃尔:那是我的土耳其蓝玉:是我还没有娶莉雅时她送给我的:就是漫山遍野的猴子,我也不肯去掉换。

屠　勃　尔　可是安东尼奥是一定完蛋了。

夏　洛　克　不,那是真的,那果真的确。去,屠勃尔,去替我找个官儿塞点钱;债据满期离现在还有两星期。我要挖他的心,要是他愆期破约;因为在威尼斯干掉了他,我能主宰整个买卖。去,去,屠勃尔,跟我在犹太寺里碰头;去,好屠勃尔;跟我在我们庙堂里相见,屠勃尔。　　　　　　　　　　　　　　　　　　　　　　　　　　[各自下。

第　二　景

[贝尔蒙。宝喜霞邸内一室]

[跋萨尼奥、宝喜霞、葛拉希阿诺、纳丽莎与侍从上。

宝　喜　霞　务必请,滞留一些时;在冒险之前,
迁延一两天,因为,您若挑错了,

I lose your company; therefore forbear a while.
There's something tells me, but it is not love,
I would not lose you; and you know yourself
Hate counsels not in such a quality.
But lest you should not understand me well, —
And yet a maiden hath no tongue but thought, —
I would detain you here some month or two
Before you venture for me. I could teach you
How to choose right, but then I am forsworn;
So will I never be; so may you miss me;
But if you do, you'll make me wish a sin,
That I had been forsworn. Beshrew your eyes,
They have o'erlook'd me and divided me:
One half of me is yours, the other half yours,
Mine own, I would say; but if mine, then yours,
And so all yours. O! these naughty times
Puts bars between the owners and their rights;
And so, though yours, not yours. Prove it so,
Let fortune go to hell for it, not I.
I speak too long, but 'tis to peise the time,
To eke it, and to draw it out in length,
To stay you from election.

Bassanio   Let me choose;
For as I am, I live upon the rack.

Portia   Upon the rack, Bassanio! Then confess
What treason there is mingled with your love.

Bassanio   None but that ugly treason of mistrust,
Which makes me fear th' enjoying of my love:
There may as well be amity and life
'Tween snow and fire as treason and my love.

Portia   Ay, but I fear you speak upon the rack,
Where men enforced do speak anything.

我将失去您的俦伴；故而，且暂慢。
我衷心感觉到，不过那不是爱情，
我不愿失掉您；而您自己也知道，
憎恶可不会作出这样的规劝。
但是，免得您对我的心情不了解，——
不过一个闺女不便说，只能想，——
在您为我冒险前，我要您逗留
一两个月的时间。我能教与您
怎样去挑选对，但那就违犯了誓言；
我可决不做：您这样也许会失掉我：
而您若失去我，我将宁愿犯罪过，
甘心发伪誓。诅咒您一双俊眼，
它们望透我，我将分成了两半；
一半是您的，另一半也还是您的。
是我自己的，我要说；但如果是我的，
也就归了您，全都属于您所有。
啊，这个刁钻的时世泼无徒，
它把所有者和他的权利分隔开！
所以，虽然是您的，却不为您所有。
要证实这件事。让命运遭殃，不是我。
我说得太久了；但只为拖时间，增加它，
延伸它，推迟您的挑选。

跋萨尼奥　　　　　　　　　让我来挑吧；
因为我此刻，像在刑台上受逼供。

宝　喜　霞　拷问台，跋萨尼奥！那么，招供出
您那情爱中可杂有叛逆之思。

跋萨尼奥　没有，只除了那猜疑恐惧的逆念，
疑惧我一片真情不能得实现：
叛逆之思同我的情爱不相容，
正如雪花和火焰没亲交两不和。

宝　喜　霞　嗳，我怕您在拷问台上作供词，
在那里受不了逼供，就胡言乱语。

Bassanio Promise me life, and I'll confess the truth.

Portia Well then, confess and live.

Bassanio   *Confess* and *love*

Had been the very sum of my confession:

O happy torment, when my torturer

Doth teach me answers for deliverance!

But let me to my fortune and the caskets.

Portia Away, then! I am lock'd in one of them:

If you do love me, you will find me out.

Nerissa and the rest, stand all aloof;

Let music sound while he doth make his choice;

Then, if he lose, he makes a swan-like end,

Fading in music: that the comparison

May stand more proper, my eye shall be the stream

And watery death-bed for him. He may win;

And what is music then? Then music is

Even as the flourish when true subjects bow

To a new-crowned monarch; such it is

As are those dulcet sounds in break of day

That creep into the dreaming bridegroom's ear

And summon him to marriage. Now he goes,

With no less presence, but with much more love,

Than young Alcides when he did redeem

The virgin tribute paid by howling Troy

To the sea-monster: I stand for sacrifice;

The rest aloof are the Dardanian wives,

With bleared visages come forth to view

The issue of th' exploit. Go, Hercules!

Live thou, I live. With much much more dismay

I view the fight than thou that mak'st the fray.

[*Music, whilst* Bassanio *comments*

on the caskets to himself.]

Song.

Tell me where is fancy bred,

跋萨尼奥　　答应让我活下去,我据实招供。

宝　喜　霞　　好呗,招认了,活着吧。

跋萨尼奥　　　　　　　　　　"招认"和"爱"
　　　　　　是我供词的全部:啊,这苦楚
　　　　　　多愉快,施刑人教了我解脱的答话!
　　　　　　但放我去面对命运和那些匣儿。

宝　喜　霞　　那么去吧! 我的像锁闭在一只匣里:
　　　　　　您若真爱我,您会找到我的像。
　　　　　　纳丽莎和其他众人,都站开些。
　　　　　　在他挑选时,将音乐鸣奏起来;
　　　　　　那样,倘使有错失,他将天鹅般
　　　　　　消逝在乐曲声中:为了使比喻
　　　　　　更确切,我一双泪眼好比是清流,
　　　　　　做他的水葬场。他也许会能得胜;
　　　　　　那时节音乐是什么? 音乐便好比
　　　　　　忠敬的臣民面对新加冕的君主,
　　　　　　鞠躬致敬时那华章的普奏;
　　　　　　又像是黎明时分那悦耳的清音
　　　　　　送进正在好梦中的新郎两耳内,
　　　　　　催他起身行嘉礼。他此刻行进着,
　　　　　　真像年轻的大力神,丰采不相差,
　　　　　　只是满腔多情爱,当他去拯救
　　　　　　哀号的特洛亚居民献给海怪的
　　　　　　那童贞处女:我便是献祭的牺牲:
　　　　　　其他人站着好比特洛亚众妇女,
　　　　　　泪眼朦胧地,出来看这场壮举
　　　　　　结局如何。去吧,大力神赫居里!
　　　　　　您能活,我也能活着:您这番武功
　　　　　　使我比您更平添许多分惊恐。

　　　　　　　〔跋萨尼奥独白评定三只匣子时,乐声鸣奏。〕

歌

　　　　告诉我爱情产生在何方,

> *Or in the heart or in the head,*
> *How begot, how nourished?*
> *Reply, reply.*
>
> *It is engend'red in the eyes,*
> *With gazing fed; and fancy dies*
> *In the cradle where it lies.*
> *Let us all ring fancy's knell:*
> *I'll begin it. — Ding, dong, bell.*

[All] *Ding, dong, bell.*

Bassanio So may the outward shows be least themselves:
The world is still deceiv'd with ornament.
In law, what plea so tainted and corrupt
But, being season'd with a gracious voice,
Obscures the show of evil? In religion,
What damned error but some sober brow
Will bless it, and approve it with a text,
Hiding the grossness with fair ornament?
There is no vice so simple but assumes
Some mark of virtue on his outward parts.
How many cowards, whose hearts are all as false
As stairs of sand, wear yet upon their chins
The beards of Hercules and frowning Mars;
Who, inward search'd, have livers white as milk;
And these assume but valour's excrement
To render them redoubted! Look on beauty
And you shall see 'tis purchas'd by the weight;
Which therein works a miracle in nature,
Making them lightest that wear most of it:
So are those crisped snaky golden locks
Which make such wanton gambols with the wind,
Upon supposed fairness, often known
To be the dowry of a second head,
The skull that bred them, in the sepulchre.

出自头脑里，还出自心房，
它怎样生殖，又怎样育养？
　　回答我，回答我。
爱情的光焰在眼中点亮，
用凝视喂饲；但迅速消亡，
它的摇篮便是它的灵床。
　　让我们把爱的丧钟敲响；
我来开始敲——叮当，叮当。

众　　人 叮当，叮当。

跋萨尼奥 故而，仅仅外表不见得是真相：
世人总会被表面的虚饰所欺蒙。
在法律地界，任何肮脏的辞讼，
只须用优雅的声音为它辩护，
哪能不隐晦罪恶的真情？宗教上，
哪一件恶毒的罪孽，不是貌似
端正，不能引经据典，曲为它
祝福、赞许，把酷烈用文饰来掩盖？
没有哪一桩邪恶简单而明了，
总在表面上装一点美德的标记：
多少个懦夫，他们的心假得像
黄沙垒成的梯子，他们下颏上
有赫居里斯和蹙额的玛斯的须髯，
向胸中检视，他们的肝胆白得
像牛奶；这些都装出勇武的威仪，
使他们显得可畏！再纵观美貌，
须知那是用美人的庄重所购置；
它在赋有者身上形成了怪异，
使那些愈是美丽的愈显得轻飘：
在风中翩跹戏跃、蛇一般的金黄
鬈发在美人额上起着波纹皱，
往往是另一个头上的覆额金云，
原本的骷髅早已长眠在地下。

Thus ornament is but the guiled shore

To a most dangerous sea; the beauteous scarf

Veiling an Indian beauty; in a word,

The seeming truth which cunning times put on

To entrap the wisest. Therefore, thou gaudy gold,

Hard food for Midas, I will none of thee;

Nor none of thee, thou pale and common drudge

'Tween man and man: but thou, thou meagre lead,

Which rather threaten'st than dost promise aught,

Thy plainness moves me more than eloquence,

And here choose I: joy be the consequence!

Portia　[*Aside.*] How all the other passions fleet to air,

As doubtful thoughts, and rash-embrac'd despair,

And shuddering fear, and green-ey'd jealousy!

O love! be moderate; allay thy ecstasy;

In measure rain thy joy; scant this excess;

I feel too much thy blessing; make it less,

For fear I surfeit!

Bassanio　　　　What find I here?

　　　　　　　　　　　[*Opening the leaden casket.*]

Fair Portia's counterfeit! What demi-god

Hath come so near creation? Move these eyes?

Or whether riding on the balls of mine,

Seem they in motion? Here are sever'd lips,

Parted with sugar breath; so sweet a bar

Should sunder such sweet friends. Here in her hairs

The painter plays the spider, and hath woven

A golden mesh t' entrap the hearts of men

Faster than gnats in cobwebs: but her eyes! —

How could he see to do them? Having made one,

Methinks it should have power to steal both his,

这样,装饰不过是诡诈的岸滩,
引人进极险的大海;或印度美人
一张美丽的面纱;一句话,它乃是
刁钻的时世用它来捕捉智者的、
那貌似的真理。故而,炫丽的黄金,
玛达斯的坚硬食物,我与你无缘,
也无取于你,人与人之间的奴仆,
苍白而下贱:可是你,贫乏的钝铅,
你有点威吓,可并不允许什么,
你这个苍白却比雄辩更能
打动我的心;我就在这里挑选定:
让结果为我欢庆!

宝　喜　霞　　[旁白]所有其他的激情都烟消云散,
比如,狐疑的设想,莽撞的绝望,
战栗的恐惧,绿眼乜斜的猜忌!
啊,爱情,
温和些;把你的狂喜镇静些微;
节制你的欢快;减轻这么多过度。
我感受你的恩幸太多了:减少些,
因为我生怕饱餍。

跋萨尼奥　　　　　　　　这里是什么?

[启铅匣。]

美好的宝喜霞的画像!什么半仙,
这么接近了神创? 这一双眼睛
在流盼? 或许,映上了我的眼珠,
它们像在移动? 双唇微启着,
中间用蜜息分隔开:这样甜的横隔,
分开了这样甜的好友。在她鬈发里,
画师像蜘蛛,撒布了金网去捕捉
才郎们的心,比蛛网捉飞虫还快:
但她的眼睛,他怎能瞧得见去描绘?
画好了一只,它便会偷掉他一双

And leave itself unfurnish'd: yet look, how far
The substance of my praise doth wrong this shadow
In underprizing it, so far this shadow
Doth limp behind the substance. Here's the scroll,
The continent and summary of my fortune.
[*Reads.*] *You that choose not by the view,*

   Chance as fair and choose as true!
   Since this fortune falls to you,
   Be content and seek no new.
   If you be well pleas'd with this,
   And hold your fortune for your bliss,
   Turn to where your lady is
   And claim her with a loving kiss.

A gentle scroll. Fair lady, by your leave; [*Kissing her.*]
I come by note, to give and to receive.
Like one of two contending in a prize,
That thinks he hath done well in people's eyes,
Hearing applause and universal shout,
Giddy in spirit, still gazing in a doubt
Whether those peals of praise be his or no;
So, thrice-fair lady, stand I, even so,
As doubtful whether what I see be true,
Until confirm'd, sign'd, ratified by you.
Portia You see me, Lord Bassanio, where I stand,
Such as I am: though for myself alone
I would not be ambitious in my wish
To wish myself much better, yet for you
I would be trebled twenty times myself,
A thousand times more fair, ten thousand times More
  rich;
That only to stand high in your account,
I might in virtues, beauties, livings, friends,
Exceed account. But the full sum of me
Is sum of something which, to term in gross,

睛光，使那画好的不能成双。
可是，瞧吧，我这些赞美的言辞
多么低估了她这个倩影，正如同
这倩影远蹩在她的真像后面。
这是个纸卷，我命运的内容和概要。
[念]你挑选不凭虚华的外表，
　　选得果然真，取的机缘妙！
　　既然这美运对你这般好，
　　心满意足吧，休得去多跑。
　　要是你对此衷心感满意，
　　将你的美运当洪福天齐，
　　走到你这位美姣娘那里，
　　招纳她用深深一吻双喜。

温柔的纸卷。多美的姑娘，请允许；[吻她。]
我凭这小帖来对您给与和收取。
像两个比武力士之中有一名，
自以为他在众人眼里很高明，
听到喝彩声和普通的喧闹，
觉得神志眩晕，凝望着不知道
那些赞赏的欢呼是真或不是；
便这般，绝色的姑娘，我站着，在此，
对我所见的是否真实我怀疑，
要等证实，承认，批准了，经过您。

宝喜霞　您见我，跋萨尼奥公子，站在此，
不过是这样一个人：虽然为自己，
我不愿存任何野心，希望自己
更好些；可是，为了您我愿自己
好上二十倍加三番，一千倍更美，
一万倍愈加富有；
为在您心目中占有个居高的品第，
我愿在修德、美貌、生计、亲友等
各方面都迈越寻常；但我的一切，

Is an unlesson'd girl, unschool'd, unpractis'd;
Happy in this, she is not yet so old
But she may learn; happier than this,
She is not bred so dull but she can learn;
Happiest of all is that her gentle spirit
Commits itself to yours to be directed,
As from her lord, her governor, her king.
Myself and what is mine to you and yours
Is now converted. But now I was the lord
Of this fair mansion, master of my servants,
Queen o'er myself; and even now, but now,
This house, these servants, and this same myself,
Are yours- my lord's. I give them with this ring,
Which when you part from, lose, or give away,
Let it presage the ruin of your love,
And be my vantage to exclaim on you.

Bassanio Madam, you have bereft me of all words,
Only my blood speaks to you in my veins;
And there is such confusion in my powers
As, after some oration fairly spoke
By a beloved prince, there doth appear
Among the buzzing pleased multitude;
Where every something, being blent together,
Turns to a wild of nothing, save of joy,
Express'd and not express'd. But when this ring
Parts from this finger, then parts life from hence:
O! then be bold to say Bassanio's dead.

Nerissa My lord and lady, it is now our time,
That have stood by and seen our wishes prosper,
To cry, good joy. Good joy, my lord and lady!

不过如此,即一个没训诲的姑娘,
无学问,无经历;好在她年纪不大,
还能够受教诲;更亏她生来不愚鲁,
还能够勤学习,最幸运是她的生性
温顺,正好仰赖您的精神所指引,
以您作为她的良人、主政和君王。
我自己和我所有的如今变成了
您的和您所有的:在此刻以前,
我是这华堂宅邸的领主,我诸多
仆从的主人,我自己一身的女王;
可是就在此一刻,这现今,这宅院,
这许多仆从,以及我自身,都成为
您所有,夫君;我用这指环给与您;
它啊,如若您离开它,把它失掉,
或送给人家,就预兆您爱情毁灭,
我那时便有权对您扬声责怪。

跋萨尼奥 姑娘,您使我失去了我所有的言辞,
我的血只在我脉管里对您鸣响;
而我的灵机呈现出这样的混乱,
正如同,当一位很受爱戴的君侯
说完了他那篇优美的演讲以后,
欢愉的群众发一阵营营的兴奋;
其中每一桩什么,跟其他相混同,
变成了什么也不是的,只是欢乐
的洪荒,表现出或者未曾被表现。
但当这指环离开了这手指,生命
也就离开了这里边:啊,那就
可以大胆说,跋萨尼奥已经死!

纳 丽 莎 姑爷和姑娘,我们本来在一边,
眼见我们的心愿圆满得辉煌,
现在轮到了我们来欢呼庆贺:
贺你们团栾欢喜春,姑爷和姑娘!

Gratiano My Lord Bassanio, and my gentle lady,
I wish you all the joy that you can wish;
For I am sure you can wish none from me;
And when your honours mean to solemnize
The bargain of your faith, I do beseech you
Even at that time I may be married too.

Bassanio With all my heart, so thou canst get a wife.

Gratiano I thank your lordship, you have got me one.
My eyes, my lord, can look as swift as yours:
You saw the mistress, I beheld the maid;
You lov'd, I lov'd; for intermission
No more pertains to me, my lord, than you.
Your fortune stood upon the caskets there,
And so did mine too, as the matter falls;
For wooing here until I sweat again,
And swearing till my very roof was dry
With oaths of love, at last, if promise last,
I got a promise of this fair one here
To have her love, provided that your fortune
Achiev'd her mistress.

Portia   Is this true, Nerissa?

Nerissa Madam, it is, so you stand pleas'd withal.

Bassanio And do you, Gratiano, mean good faith?

Gratiano Yes, faith, my lord.

Bassanio Our feast shall be much honour'd in your marriage.

Gratiano We'll play with them the first boy for a thousand ducats.

Nerissa What! and stake down?

Gratiano No; we shall ne'er win at that sport, and stake
down.
But who comes here? Lorenzo and his infidel?
What, and my old Venetian friend, Salanio!

[*Enter* Lorenzo, Jessica, *and* Salanio, a Messenger from
Venice.]

Bassanio Lorenzo and Salanio, welcome hither,

葛拉希阿诺	跋萨尼奥公子,温柔的嫂夫人,
	我愿你们有你们所愿有的欢喜:
	因为我深知你们多,我决不会少:
	当你们二位决定要什么时候
	举行燕尔新婚礼,我请求你们,
	我在那时节,也要完婚成燕好。
跋 萨 尼 奥	我完全赞成,只要你能找到个妻子。
葛拉希阿诺	我感谢你仁君,你为我已找到了一位。
	我这双眼睛能瞧得跟你一样快:
	你看中主小娘,我瞧中她的小伴娘;
	你爱得迅速,我同样也爱得爽朗。
	懒散和间断对于你我都无缘。
	你的命运仗赖在那只匣儿上,
	我的也同样,经过情形就如此;
	因为我在此求情说爱出大汗,
	指天咒誓一直到喉舌尽干焦,
	最后,如果允诺还算数,她答应
	只要你能有运得到她主人,
	我也能得到她的爱。
宝 喜 霞	真的吗,纳丽莎?
纳 丽 莎	姑娘,正是,如果您乐意这么样。
跋 萨 尼 奥	那你,葛拉希阿诺,是诚心诚意的吗?
葛拉希阿诺	是的,当真,仁君。
跋 萨 尼 奥	我们的欢宴将因你们的婚礼
	而更加光荣。
葛拉希阿诺	我们跟他们打赌,先养第一个
	男孩的赢得一千块金特格。
纳 丽 莎	什么,押下赌注吗?
葛拉希阿诺	不;要是下赌注,我们决不会赢。
	可是谁来了?洛良佐和他的邪教徒?
	嗨,还有我威尼斯老友萨勒里奥?
	〔洛良佐、絜雪格与萨勒里奥及一威城来的使者上。
跋 萨 尼 奥	洛良佐和萨勒里奥,欢迎你们来;

If that the youth of my new interest here
Have power to bid you welcome. By your leave,
I bid my very friends and countrymen,
Sweet Portia, welcome.

Portia　　　　　So do I, my lord;
They are entirely welcome.

Lorenzo　I thank your honour. For my part, my lord,
My purpose was not to have seen you here;
But meeting with Salanio by the way,
He did entreat me, past all saying nay,
To come with him along.

Salanio　　　　　I did, my lord,
And I have reason for it. Signior Antonio
Commends him to you.

　　　　　[*Gives* Bassanio *a letter*]

Bassanio　　　　　Ere I ope his letter,
I pray you tell me how my good friend doth.

Salanio　Not sick, my lord, unless it be in mind;
Nor well, unless in mind; his letter there
Will show you his estate.

Gratiano　Nerissa, cheer yon stranger; bid her welcome.
Your hand, Salanio. What's the news from Venice?
How doth that royal merchant, good Antonio?
I know he will be glad of our success:
We are the Jasons, we have won the fleece.

Salanio　I would you had won the fleece that he hath lost.

Portia　There are some shrewd contents in yon same pa-
　　per.
That steal the colour from Bassanio's cheek:
Some dear friend dead, else nothing in the world
Could turn so much the constitution
Of any constant man. What, worse and worse!
With leave, Bassanio: I am half yourself,

我自己,也是新来乍到,若是我
有权欢迎你们来。经您的同意,
亲密的宝喜霞,我欢迎我的朋友
和同乡到此来。

宝 喜 霞　　　　　　　我也欢迎,夫君,
衷心欢迎他们来。

洛 良 佐　多谢阁下。我原先,公子,不是
想到这里来拜访;可是在路上
碰到萨勒里奥,他却是硬邀我
不容分说,同他一起来。

萨 勒 里 奥　　　　　　　　我确是
勉强他,公子;我有因由这么干。
安东尼奥舍人嘱咐我代致意。

[给跋萨尼奥一信。]

跋 萨 尼 奥　我在打开他这信之前,要请您
告诉我我的好友怎么样。

萨 勒 里 奥　　　　　　　　　没有病,
公子,除了在心里;也不好,除了
在心里:那封信会告您他的真情。

葛 拉 希 阿 诺　纳丽莎,招待那位客人;欢迎她。
把手伸给我,萨勒里奥:威尼斯
有什么新闻? 那位经商巨子
怎么样,慷慨的安东尼奥舍人?
我知道他会为我们的成功高兴;
我们是鉴逊,我们觅得了金羊毛。

萨 勒 里 奥　但愿你们觅得了他失掉的金羊毛。

宝 喜 霞　那张柬帖上有招致烦恼的凶讯,
它引得跋萨尼奥脸色变苍白:
许因亲爱的朋友死掉了;否则
没有别的事能这么震撼一个
正常男子的身心。什么,更坏了!
允许我,跋萨尼奥;妻是夫之半,

And I must freely have the half of anything
That this same paper brings you.

Bassanio   O sweet Portia!
Here are a few of the unpleasant'st words
That ever blotted paper. Gentle lady,
When I did first impart my love to you,
I freely told you all the wealth I had
Ran in my veins, I was a gentleman;
And then I told you true. And yet, dear lady,
Rating myself at nothing, you shall see
How much I was a braggart. When I told you
My state was nothing, I should then have told you
That I was worse than nothing; for indeed
I have engag'd myself to a dear friend,
Engag'd my friend to his mere enemy,
To feed my means. Here is a letter, lady,
The paper as the body of my friend,
And every word in it a gaping wound
Issuing life-blood. But is it true, Salanio?
Hath all his ventures fail'd? What, not one hit?
From Tripolis, from Mexico, and England,
From Lisbon, Barbary, and India?
And not one vessel scape the dreadful touch
Of merchant-marring rocks?

Salanio   Not one, my lord.
Besides, it should appear that, if he had
The present money to discharge the Jew,
He would not take it. Never did I know
A creature that did bear the shape of man,
So keen and greedy to confound a man.
He plies the duke at morning and at night,
And doth impeach the freedom of the state,

我一定得知晓这张纸帖儿带给您
任何东西的一半。

跋萨尼奥　　　　　　　　亲密的宝喜霞，
这儿有自来涂抹到纸上的最痛彻
人心的几句话！温良的姑娘，当我
最初面向您倾吐我爱慕的时分，
我坦白告诉您，我全部财富都在我
血管中流注，我是一个士君子；
当时我说的是实话：可是，好姑娘，
将我自己说成无财富，您须知
我却夸了多么大的口。我告您
我境况清贫时，我那时应当告您
我还比清贫远不如；因为，果真的，
我让我自己亏累了一位至友，
又叫这至友亏欠了他的仇家，
为替我筹款。这儿有封信，姑娘，
这纸张好比正是我至友的身体，
上面每个字都是开裂的创口，
流着生命血。真的吗，萨勒里奥？
他所有的投资全毁了？没一桩成功？
从屈黎波里、墨西哥、英格兰回来，
还有从里斯本、巴巴利、印度回来？
没有一条海舶逃过了那摧毁
商船的礁石的骇人撞击吗？

萨勒里奥　　　　　　　　　　一条
都没有，公子。何况，事态显然是，
假使他有现款去打发犹太佬，
那家伙也不肯接受。我从未见过
一个家伙，样子像是人，深心里
却贪残狠毒得定要消灭人家：
他没早没晚促迫着公爵去执法，
并且诘责威尼斯城邦有没有

If they deny him justice. Twenty merchants,
The duke himself, and the magnificoes
Of greatest port, have all persuaded with him;
But none can drive him from the envious plea
Of forfeiture, of justice, and his bond.

Jessica　When I was with him, I have heard him swear
To Tubal and to Chus, his countrymen,
That he would rather have Antonio's flesh
Than twenty times the value of the sum
That he did owe him; and I know, my lord,
If law, authority, and power, deny not,
It will go hard with poor Antonio.

Portia　Is it your dear friend that is thus in trouble?

Bassanio　The dearest friend to me, the kindest man,
The best condition'd and unwearied spirit
In doing courtesies; and one in whom
The ancient Roman honour more appears
Than any that draws breath in Italy.

Portia　What sum owes he the Jew?

Bassanio　For me, three thousand ducats.

Portia　　　　　　　　　　　　　　　　What! no more?
Pay him six thousand, and deface the bond;
Double six thousand, and then treble that,
Before a friend of this description
Shall lose a hair through Bassanio's fault.
First go with me to church and call me wife,
And then away to Venice to your friend;
For never shall you lie by Portia's side
With an unquiet soul. You shall have gold
To pay the petty debt twenty times over:
When it is paid, bring your true friend along.
My maid Nerissa and myself meantime,

　　　　　　自由，倘使他们不给他行公道：
　　　　　　二十位大商家，公爵自己，还有
　　　　　　最负声望的显贵，都曾劝过他；
　　　　　　可是没有人能使他收回辞讼，
　　　　　　他坚持要求按立约处罚、执法。
絜　雪　格　我在家里时曾听得他对屠勃尔
　　　　　　和楚斯，他的两个同族人，发过誓，
　　　　　　说他宁愿有安东尼奥的身上肉，
　　　　　　不愿有二十倍借款那么多的钱：
　　　　　　我知道，贵公子，倘使法律、权威
　　　　　　和权力不能否定他的要求的话，
　　　　　　可怜的安东尼奥怕劫数难逃。
宝　喜　霞　您那位亲爱的朋友在这般遭难吗？
跋萨尼奥　我最亲爱的朋友，最温蔼的人，
　　　　　　一位品德真高超、极慷慨仁和，
　　　　　　肝胆照人的士君子，在他胸臆中
　　　　　　古罗马的光荣磊落精神辉耀得
　　　　　　比目今意大利任何人都更显焕。
宝　喜　霞　他欠那犹太人多大一笔款子？
跋萨尼奥　为了我，三千金特格。
宝　喜　霞　　　　　　　　　什么，只此吗？
　　　　　　还他六千块，把那债约撤销掉，
　　　　　　六千加一倍，那数目再翻上三番，
　　　　　　也休得叫这样人品的一位朋友，
　　　　　　因跋萨尼奥的过错少一根毛发。
　　　　　　先同我去到教堂里结成夫妇，
　　　　　　再就到威尼斯去看您的朋友，
　　　　　　如果怀着颗不安的心灵，您切莫
　　　　　　躺在宝喜霞身旁。您将有比那
　　　　　　些些借款多上二十倍的金元
　　　　　　去还债：事完后，请您的挚友同来。
　　　　　　我的这伴娘纳丽莎和我自己

Will live as maids and widows. Come, away!

For you shall hence upon your wedding day.

Bid your friends welcome, show a merry cheer;

Since you are dear bought, I will love you dear.

But let me hear the letter of your friend.

Bassanio　[*Reads.*]　*Sweet Bassanio, my ships have all*
miscarried, my creditors grow cruel, my estate is
very low, my bond to the Jew is forfeit; and since,
in paying it, it is impossible I should live, all debts
are clear'd between you and I, if I might but see you
at my death. Notwithstanding, use your pleasure;
if your love do not persuade you to come, let not my
letter.

Portia　O love, dispatch all business and be gone!

Bassanio　Since I have your good leave to go away,

I will make haste; but, till I come again,

No bed shall e'er be guilty of my stay,

Nor rest be interposer 'twixt us twain.

[*Exeunt.*]

SCENE III. Venice. *A street*

[*Enter* Shylock, Salarino, Antonio, *and* Gaoler.]

Shylock　Gaoler, look to him. Tell not me of mercy;

This is the fool that lent out money gratis:

Gaoler, look to him.

Antonio　　　　　　Hear me yet, good Shylock.

Shylock　I'll have my bond; speak not against my bond.

I have sworn an oath that I will have my bond.

Thou call'dst me dog before thou hadst a cause,

But, since I am a dog, beware my fangs;

　　　　　　将如闺女、孤孀般度着时光。
　　　　　　来吧,去来。今天,在新婚的吉日,
　　　　　　您就得离开:欢迎您几位朋友,
　　　　　　要显得心情欢快:我们这姻缘
　　　　　　既然出了这么多代价,我定将
　　　　　　对您更恩爱。让我听您的朋友
　　　　　　这封信。

跋萨尼奥　　[念信]挚爱的跋萨尼奥,我的船舶悉数出了事,我的
　　　　　　债权人心怀残暴,我境况危殆,我对那犹太人的债务
　　　　　　因失约必须受罚抵偿;既然我偿付后无法幸存,你我
　　　　　　之间的债务就一笔勾销,我只盼能在临死前见你一
　　　　　　面。虽然如此,要趁你高兴:若是你的爱侣不劝你
　　　　　　来,别让我这封信劝你。

宝喜霞　　　啊,心爱的,把一切事办好,马上去!

跋萨尼奥　　我既然有您的允许速即离开,
　　　　　　我便得赶快:但在我回来之前,
　　　　　　我将不在这里哪一张床上呆,
　　　　　　您我来不及一块儿得到共休眠。

　　　　　　　　　　　　　　　　　　　　[同下。

第 三 景

　　　　　　[威尼斯。一街道]
　　　　　　[夏洛克、萨勒里诺、安东尼奥与狱卒上。

夏洛克　　　狱官,看住他:别跟我说什么仁慈;
　　　　　　这是个傻瓜,他出借款子不收息;
　　　　　　狱官,看住他。

安东尼奥　　　　　　　　再听我一声,夏洛克。

夏洛克　　　我要执行那债券;不许反对它:
　　　　　　我已经发过誓,非照约实行不可。
　　　　　　你没有理由平白地骂我是条狗;
　　　　　　既然我是狗,要小心我的狗牙:

The Duke shall grant me justice. I do wonder,
Thou naughty gaoler, that thou art so fond
To come abroad with him at his request.

Antonio   I pray thee hear me speak.

Shylock   I'll have my bond. I will not hear thee speak;
I'll have my bond; and therefore speak no more.
I'll not be made a soft and dull-eyed fool,
To shake the head, relent, and sigh, and yield
To Christian intercessors. Follow not;
I'll have no speaking; I will have my bond.

[*Exit.*]

Salarino   It is the most impenetrable cur
That ever kept with men.

Antonio   Let him alone;
I'll follow him no more with bootless prayers.
He seeks my life; his reason well I know:
I oft deliver'd from his forfeitures
Many that have at times made moan to me;
Therefore he hates me.

Salarino   I am sure the Duke
Will never grant this forfeiture to hold.

Antonio   The Duke cannot deny the course of law;
For the commodity that strangers have
With us in Venice, if it be denied,
'Twill much impeach the justice of the state,
Since that the trade and profit of the city
Consisteth of all nations. Therefore, go;
These griefs and losses have so bated me
That I shall hardly spare a pound of flesh
To-morrow to my bloody creditor.
Well, gaoler, on; pray God Bassanio come
To see me pay his debt, and then I care not.

[*Exeunt.*]

                        公爵一定会给我主持公道的，
                        你这个泼赖的狱官实在太糊涂，
                        经他的请求，放他出来这么走。
安 东 尼 奥　　我请你听我说。
夏 洛 克　　我要按立约实行，不听你的话：
                        我要按立约实行，故而莫多说。
                        我不会给弄成一个软心肠、
                        愁眉苦脸的傻瓜，摇头，发慈悲，
                        叹息着，对一些耶稣教仲裁人屈服。
                        别跟着；我不听瞎说：按立约实行。　　　〔下。
萨 拉 里 诺　　这是条人间最铁石心肠的恶狗。
安 东 尼 奥　　由他去，我将不再用不济的哀求
                        跟踪他。他要我的命；我知道那因由：
                        不少人失约还不出借款要藉没，
                        对我来诉苦，好多次我救了他们；
                        他因而恨我。
萨 拉 里 诺　　　　　　　　我信公爵决不会
                        维持这罚则。
安 东 尼 奥　　　　　　　　公爵可不能否定
                        这法律程序：因为通商的便利，
                        异邦人在我们威尼斯这里所享的，
                        若遭到否定，会损害它公道的令名，
                        而我们城邦的商业繁荣和富庶，
                        须指望诸邦众国。故而，且去吧：
                        这些悲伤、损失弄得我好衰弱，
                        只怕我明天身上匀不出一磅肉，
                        去满足我那个血腥债主的需要。
                        狱官，走吧。求上帝，让跋萨尼奥来
                        瞧我还他的债，我死也无所谓！

                                                            〔同下。

SCENE IV. Belmont. *A room in Portia's house.*

[*Enter* Portia, Nerissa, Lorenzo,
Jessica, *and* Balthasar.]

Lorenzo Madam, although I speak it in your presence,
You have a noble and a true conceit
Of godlike amity, which appears most strongly
In bearing thus the absence of your lord.
But if you knew to whom you show this honour,
How true a gentleman you send relief,
How dear a lover of my lord your husband,
I know you would be prouder of the work
Than customary bounty can enforce you.
Portia I never did repent for doing good,
Nor shall not now; for in companions
That do converse and waste the time together,
Whose souls do bear an equal yoke of love,
There must be needs a like proportion
Of lineaments, of manners, and of spirit,
Which makes me think that this Antonio,
Being the bosom lover of my lord,
Must needs be like my lord. If it be so,
How little is the cost I have bestowed
In purchasing the semblance of my soul
From out the state of hellish cruelty!
This comes too near the praising of myself;
Therefore, no more of it; hear other things.
Lorenzo, I commit into your hands
The husbandry and manage of my house
Until my lord's return; for mine own part,
I have toward heaven breath'd a secret vow
To live in prayer and contemplation,
Only attended by Nerissa here,

第 四 景

[贝尔蒙。宝喜霞邸内一室]
[宝喜霞、纳丽莎、洛良佐、絜雪格与鲍尔萨什同上。

洛 良 佐　夫人，虽然我当着您的面说话，
　　　　　您确有天神一般的亲仁高贵
　　　　　而真诚的心；而在这件事情上
　　　　　最显焕，您敦劝新婚的夫婿离家门。
　　　　　可您若知道您对谁显示这尊荣，
　　　　　对怎样一位高人君子施救助，
　　　　　他是贵公子您外子多亲密的好友，
　　　　　我知道您会更感到自豪，因做了
　　　　　比通常的宽弘义举更高朗的事。

宝 喜 霞　我从来不曾行了义举而悔恨，
　　　　　现在也不会。在知心的伴侣之间，
　　　　　经常开怀偕畅叙，相处共朝夕，
　　　　　彼此的灵魂承载着相同的爱慕，
　　　　　他们定必在相貌、风采、精神上
　　　　　有几分相同或相似；这使我想到
　　　　　这安东尼奥舍人，我夫君的挚友，
　　　　　定必同我的夫君差不多。倘如此，
　　　　　我付出的代价就显得何等渺小，
　　　　　去营救跟我的灵魂相仿佛的人，
　　　　　脱离他那地狱般惨酷的遭遇！
　　　　　但这太近于自我标榜的失态了；
　　　　　故而不必再多讲：且谈些别的事。
　　　　　洛良佐，我委托与您的执掌之中，
　　　　　我这邸宅的管理和区处，直到
　　　　　我夫君作回程：至于我自己，我对天
　　　　　曾起过密誓，要以祈祷和冥想
　　　　　度晨昏，只由纳丽莎一人伴随我，

Until her husband and my lord's return.
There is a monastery two miles off,
And there we will abide. I do desire you
Not to deny this imposition,
The which my love and some necessity
Now lays upon you.

Lorenzo   Madam, with all my heart
I shall obey you in an fair commands.

Portia   My people do already know my mind,
And will acknowledge you and Jessica
In place of Lord Bassanio and myself.
So fare you well till we shall meet again.

Lorenzo   Fair thoughts and happy hours attend on you!

Jessica   I wish your ladyship all heart's content.

Portia   I thank you for your wish, and am well pleas'd
To wish it back on you. Fare you well, Jessica.

                              [*Exeunt* Jessica *and* Lorenzo.]

Now, Balthasar,
As I have ever found thee honest-true,
So let me find thee still. Take this same letter,
And use thou all th' endeavour of a man
In speed to Padua; see thou render this
Into my cousin's hands, Doctor Bellario;
And look what notes and garments he doth give thee,
Bring them, I pray thee, with imagin'd speed
Unto the traject, to the common ferry
Which trades to Venice. Waste no time in words,
But get thee gone; I shall be there before thee.

Balthasar   Madam, I go with all convenient speed.

                                        [*Exit.*]

Portia   Come on, Nerissa, I have work in hand
That you yet know not of; we'll see our husbands
Before they think of us.

Nerissa   Shall they see us?

待到她丈夫和我的夫君归来时：
离此间两英里有一所修道的庄院；
我们将在那壁厢居住。希望您
不要推拒我这一委任的负荷；
这是我的敬爱之忱和某种需要
所对您的恳托。

洛 良 佐　　　　　　　夫人，我一心奉命；
我将遵从您一切的清明指示。

宝 喜 霞　我的家人们都已知道我的意思，
他们都会接受您和大嫂絜雪格，
来代表跋萨尼奥贵公子和我。
祝你们平安，等到我们再见时。

洛 良 佐　愿美好的神思、欢乐的时刻相随护！

絜 雪 格　我愿您夫人一切都如意，祝万福。

宝 喜 霞　多谢你们的祝福，我愿把它们
回敬给你们：日后再见了，絜雪格。

　　　　　　　　　　　　［洛良佐与絜雪格同下。

我说，鲍尔萨什，
我一向知道你诚实可靠，所以
我指望你仍然如此。取了这封信，
尽你最大的能耐火速到帕度亚，
送交给我表兄培拉里奥博士；
注意，他将有什么柬帖和衣服
交给你，你接下便得飞快到渡头；
就乘上前往威尼斯的公共渡船。
别费时说话了，就走：我将赶先到。

鲍 尔 萨 什　姑娘，我将尽快去赶路就是了。　　　［下。

宝 喜 霞　来呀，纳丽莎，我手头有事你还
不知道：我们会见到我们的丈夫，
在他们能想到我们之前。

纳 丽 莎　　　　　　　　　　他们
可会见到我们吗？

Portia   They shall, Nerissa; but in such a habit
That they shall think we are accomplished
With that we lack. I'll hold thee any wager,
When we are both accoutred like young men,
I'll prove the prettier fellow of the two,
And wear my dagger with the braver grace,
And speak between the change of man and boy
With a reed voice; and turn two mincing steps
Into a manly stride; and speak of frays
Like a fine bragging youth; and tell quaint lies,
How honourable ladies sought my love,
Which I denying, they fell sick and died;
I could not do withal. Then I'll repent,
And wish for all that, that I had not kill'd them.
And twenty of these puny lies I'll tell,
That men shall swear I have discontinu'd school
About a twelvemonth. I have within my mind
A thousand raw tricks of these bragging Jacks,
Which I will practise.
Nerissa   Why, shall we turn to men?
Portia   Fie, what a question's that,
If thou wert near a lewd interpreter!
But come, I'll tell thee all my whole device
When I am in my coach, which stays for us
At the park gate; and therefore haste away,
For we must measure twenty miles to-day.

                                    [*Exeunt.*]

宝 喜 霞　　　　　　　　　会的,纳丽莎;
但我们将穿着那样的衣装,使他们
分辨不出我们的本来面目。
我跟你打怎样的赌都行,当我们
两人都装扮成了青年汉子时,
我将会是个出脱得更俊的人儿,
身旁佩着短剑更风采奕奕,
开腔说话时带着从少年转变为
成人的芦管声,把两个袅娜小步
并成一个跟跄男子步,说起斗殴来,
活像个吹擂夸口的郎君,还编些
离奇的谎话,说什么大家的贵千金
恋上了我了,我不要,她们便害了相思
而死去;我不能去要;我跟着后悔了,
倒愿意,虽然已如此,还是莫害得
她们死;我要撒二十个这样的谎,
于是人们将赌咒,说我走出
学校门不过一年多。我记着这些
吹牛子弟们上千个不更事的伎俩,
我要拿出来搬演。

纳 丽 莎　　　　　　　怎么,我们要
变成男人吗?

宝 喜 霞　　　　　　　呸,亏你问出来,
你倒几乎成了个淫荡的通事!
可是来吧,我在四轮马车里,那等在
邸园大门口,会讲给你听我整个
计划;故而,让我们快快上程途,
我们今天得要赶二十英里路。

　　　　　　　　　　　　　　　　[同下。

SCENE V. *The same. A garden.*

[*Enter* Launcelot *and* Jessica.]

Launcelot   Yes, truly; for, look you, the sins of the father
are to be laid upon the children; therefore, I promise
you, I fear you. I was always plain with you, and so now
I speak my agitation of the matter; therefore be of good
cheer, for truly I think you are damn'd. There is but one
hope in it that can do you any good, and that is but a kind
of bastard hope neither.

Jessica   And what hope is that, I pray thee?

Launcelot   Marry, you may partly hope that your father
got you not, that you are not the Jew's daughter.

Jessica   That were a kind of bastard hope indeed; so the
sins of my mother should be visited upon me.

Launcelot   Truly then I fear you are damn'd both by father and mother; thus when I shun Scylla, your father, I fall into Charybdis, your mother; well, you
are gone both ways.

Jessica   I shall be saved by my husband; he hath made me
a Christian.

Launcelot   Truly, the more to blame he; we were Christians
enow before, e'en as many as could well live one by another. This making of Christians will raise the price of
hogs; if we grow all to be pork-eaters, we shall not
shortly have a rasher on the coals for money.

Jessica   I'll tell my husband, Launcelot, what you say;
here he comes.

[*Enter* Lorenzo.]

Lorenzo   I shall grow jealous of you shortly, Launcelot, if
you thus get my wife into corners.

Jessica   Nay, you need nor fear us, Lorenzo; Launcelot
and I are out; he tells me flatly there's no mercy for
me in heaven, because I am a Jew's daughter; and he
says you are no good member of the commonwealth,

第 五 景

[同前。花园内]

[朗斯洛忒与絜雪格上。

朗斯洛忒 是的,当真;因为,你瞧,老子的罪孽会下落到孩子们身上:所以,我管保你逃不了要遭殃。我一向跟你说老实话,所以现在同你讲了替你担忧的事:所以开怀吧,我确是认定你会进地狱。只有一个希望对你或许能有利;不过那只是不正当的希望。

絜 雪 格 那是个什么希望呢,请问?

朗 斯 洛 忒 凭玛丽,你可以有点希望,就是你父亲没有生你出来,你不是那犹太人的女儿。

絜 雪 格 那倒真是个不正当的希望了:不过那样一来我妈的罪孽就要落到我身上了。

朗 斯 洛 忒 真的,我就怕你会给你的爸和妈一块儿镇到地狱里去:便这样,避开了锡拉,你父亲这块大礁石,却给卷进了却列勃迪斯你母亲这个大旋涡里去:好,你从两方面都不得超生。

絜 雪 格 我将因我的丈夫而得救;他把我变成了个基督教徒。

朗 斯 洛 忒 真是,他这下子可罪责难逃:我们基督教徒原本是够多的了;多到已经满满的,还好活得下去,这个挨着那个的。这么增添基督教徒会叫猪肉涨价;倘使我们都成了吃猪肉的,不久我们会出了钱买不到一片煎咸肉哩。

絜 雪 格 我要告诉我丈夫,朗斯洛忒,你说的是什么话;他来了。

[洛良佐上。

洛 良 佐 我不久要对你吃起醋来,朗斯洛忒,你若这样将我妻子挤到壁角里去。

絜 雪 格 不,你不用害怕,洛良佐:朗斯洛忒跟我在吵架。他干脆跟我说,上天不会给我仁慈,因为我是个犹太人的女儿;他又说,你不是个咱们国家的好公民,

for in converting Jews to Christians you raise the price
of pork.

Lorenzo I shall answer that better to the commonwealth
than you can the getting up of the negro's belly; the
Moor is with child by you, Launcelot.

Launcelot It is much that the Moor should be more than
reason; but if she be less than an honest woman, she
is indeed more than I took her for.

Lorenzo How every fool can play upon the word! I think the
best grace of wit will shortly turn into silence, and dis-
course grow commendable in none only but parrots. Go
in, sirrah; bid them prepare for dinner.

Launcelot That is done, sir; they have all stomachs.

Lorenzo Goodly Lord, what a wit-snapper are you! Then
bid them prepare dinner.

Launcelot That is done too, sir, only *cover* is the word.

Lorenzo Will you cover, then, sir?

Launcelot Not so, sir, neither; I know my duty.

Lorenzo Yet more quarrelling with occasion! Wilt thou
show the whole wealth of thy wit in an instant? I pray
thee understand a plain man in his plain meaning: go
to thy fellows, bid them cover the table, serve in the
meat, and we will come in to dinner.

Launcelot For the table, sir, it shall be served in; for the
meat, sir, it shall be covered; for your coming in to
dinner, sir, why, let it be as humours and conceits
shall govern.   [*Exit.*]

Lorenzo O dear discretion, how his words are suited!
The fool hath planted in his memory
An army of good words; and I do know
A many fools that stand in better place,
Garnish'd like him, that for a tricksy word
Defy the matter. How cheer'st thou, Jessica?
And now, good sweet, say thy opinion,
How dost thou like the Lord Bassanio's wife?

Jessica Past all expressing. It is very meet
The Lord Bassanio live an upright life,

因为你把犹太人变成了基督教徒,你叫猪肉涨了价。

洛　良　佐　为那件事我能对国家答话,要比你为弄大那黑姑娘
　　　　　的肚子能对国家答话,容易得多哩:你叫那摩阿女孩
　　　　　儿怀了孕呢,朗斯洛忒。

朗斯洛忒　那个摩阿女的肚子里多那么一层道理,固然是多哩;
　　　　　可是她若是个不怎么规矩的娘们,她才果真是出乎
　　　　　我的意料之外。

洛　良　佐　怎么每一个呆子都会嚼舌头贫嘴! 我想过不了多久,
　　　　　聪明才智的最好风致将会沉默了,而说话只对于鹦鹉
　　　　　才是可以赞许的。你去! 那么,要他们准备开饭吧。

朗斯洛忒　那已准备好了,您家;他们都有好胃口。

洛　良　佐　老天爷,你这巧舌如簧的傢伙,那就让他们准备
　　　　　开饭。

朗斯洛忒　那也准备好了,您家;只要说一声"铺上"就是。

洛　良　佐　那么,你就铺上吗,您家?

朗斯洛忒　不敢,您家;我懂得本份。

洛　良　佐　还是那么咬文嚼字贫嘴! 你是要在顷刻间把你全部
　　　　　的聪明才智都使出来吗? 我关照你,要懂得一个老
　　　　　实人说他的老实话:去跟你那些伙伴们讲,要他们把
　　　　　桌子铺上,把肉端出来,我们要进来吃饭了。

朗斯洛忒　桌子,您家,是要摆上的;肉,您家,是要端上的;关于
　　　　　您进来饭的事,您家,唔,让它由兴致和奇想去决
　　　　　定吧。　　　　　　　　　　　　　　　　　〔下。

洛　良　佐　啊,慎思明辨,他的话多机灵!
　　　　　这丑角在他记忆里配备了多么
　　　　　齐整的一套字眼;而我也知道,
　　　　　有许多丑角,比他站得地位高,
　　　　　修饰得同他一个样,胡扯起来
　　　　　叫人什么也不懂。你怎样,絜雪格?
　　　　　现在,心爱的好人儿,且说说你觉得
　　　　　跋萨尼奥公子这新娘怎么样?

絜　雪　格　好到说不尽。依我看,真是该这位
　　　　　跋萨尼奥贵公子品德两高超;

For, having such a blessing in his lady,

He finds the joys of heaven here on earth;

And if on earth he do not merit it,

In reason he should never come to heaven.

Why, if two gods should play some heavenly match,

And on the wager lay two earthly women,

And Portia one, there must be something else

Pawn'd with the other; for the poor rude world

Hath not her fellow.

Lorenzo   Even such a husband

Hast thou of me as she is for a wife.

Jessica   Nay, but ask my opinion too of that.

Lorenzo   I will anon; first let us go to dinner.

Jessica   Nay, let me praise you while I have a stomach.

Lorenzo   No, pray thee, let it serve for table-talk;

Then howsoe'er thou speak'st, 'mong other things

I shall digest it.

Jessica   Well, I'll set you forth.

                                        [*Exeunt.*]

在他这媳妇身上天恩这般大，
他简直在地上享着天上的洪福；
而若在地上他不求这一份天恩，
按理他将来会要上不了天堂。
嗨呀，假使有两位天神去赌赛，
当作赌注，押两个人间的女子，
一边押上了宝喜霞，那一边就得
另押上一位女娘，因为这可怜
寒伧的人世间没她的对手。

洛　良　佐　　　　　　　　　　　　　我便是
你的这样个丈夫，正如她是个妻。

絮　雪　格　且慢，也来问问我有何意见。

洛　良　佐　我就要问你：首先，让我们吃饭。

絮　雪　格　且慢，在我还有胃口时称赞你。

洛　良　佐　且不，请你，我们一边吃，一边谈，
那时候，不论你怎样讲，我都可以
吞下去一起消化。

絮　雪　格　　　　　　　　　好吧，我来讲。

〔同下。

ACT IV.

SCENE I. Venice. *A court of justice*

⌈*Enter the* Duke; *the* Magnificoes; Antonio, Bassanio,
Gratiano, Salarino, Salanio, *and Others.* ⌉

Duke   What, is Antonio here?

Antonio   Ready, so please your Grace.

Duke   I am sorry for thee; thou art come to answer
A stony adversary, an inhuman wretch,
Uncapable of pity, void and empty
From any dram of mercy.

Antonio   I have heard
Your Grace hath ta'en great pains to qualify
His rigorous course; but since he stands obdurate,
And that no lawful means can carry me
Out of his envy's reach, I do oppose
My patience to his fury, and am arm'd
To suffer with a quietness of spirit
The very tyranny and rage of his.

Duke   Go one, and call the Jew into the court.

Salarino   He is ready at the door; he comes, my lord.

⌈*Enter* Shylock. ⌉

Duke   Make room, and let him stand before our face.
Shylock, the world thinks, and I think so too,
That thou but leadest this fashion of thy malice

第 四 幕

第 一 景

［威尼斯。一法庭］

［公爵，众显贵、安东尼奥、跋萨尼奥、葛拉希阿诺、萨勒里奥及其他人等上。

公　　爵 喂，安东尼奥在这里吗？

安 东 尼 奥 有，回贵爵阁下。

公　　爵 我为你扼腕；你来跟一个狠心肠
对手对质，他是个没怜悯、空无
一点儿仁慈，不近人情的恶棍。

安 东 尼 奥 我听说阁下已费尽心思去缓和
他的凶横；但既然他顽固不化，
又无合法的手段可救我逸出他
怨毒的罗网，我只能用忍耐对付
他那股狂怒，以镇静的精神自卫，
去忍受他的残暴，他那阵疯魔。

公　　爵 下去一个人，传那犹太人上庭来。

萨 勒 里 诺 他在庭门口等着：他来了，贵爵。

　　　　　　　　　　　　［夏洛克上。

公　　爵 让开些，容他站立着面对我们。
夏洛克，人们这么忖，我也这么想，
你只是故意装这副凶恶的态势，

To the last hour of act; and then, 'tis thought,
Thou'lt show thy mercy and remorse, more strange
Than is thy strange apparent cruelty;
And where thou now exacts the penalty, —
Which is a pound of this poor merchant's flesh, —
Thou wilt not only loose the forfeiture,
But, touch'd with human gentleness and love,
Forgive a moiety of the principal,
Glancing an eye of pity on his losses,
That have of late so huddled on his back,
Enow to press a royal merchant down,
And pluck commiseration of his state
From brassy bosoms and rough hearts of flint,
From stubborn Turks and Tartars, never train'd
To offices of tender courtesy.
We all expect a gentle answer, Jew.
Shylock I have possess'd your Grace of what I purpose,
And by our holy Sabbath have I sworn
To have the due and forfeit of my bond.
If you deny it, let the danger light
Upon your charter and your city's freedom.
You'll ask me why I rather choose to have
A weight of carrion flesh than to receive
Three thousand ducats. I'll not answer that,
But say it is my humour: is it answer'd?
What if my house be troubled with a rat,
And I be pleas'd to give ten thousand ducats
To have it ban'd? What, are you answer'd yet?
Some men there are love not a gaping pig;
Some that are mad if they behold a cat;
And others, when the bagpipe sings i' the nose,
Cannot contain their urine; for affection,
Mistress of passion, sways it to the mood

直到那最后关头；这下子都以为，
你会显你的仁慈和恻隐，这却比
你那表面上的残酷更出人意外；
到现在你虽然坚持要照约处罚，
宰割这可怜的商家身上一磅肉，
可是在最后，你将不仅放弃掉
那处罚，还因为受到人情的恺悌
和仁爱所感动，让掉一部分本金；
你会用怜悯的眼光看他的亏耗，
这些近来都不断乱堆到他背上，
足可把一个巨商压倒在地上，
使黄铜的胸怀和燧石的心肠，
使刚愎的土耳其、剽悍的鞑靼犷蛮，
他们从不知什么温存慈惠，
也会对他的际遇起哀怜和恻隐。
我们都指望你有个和蔼的回答。

夏　洛　克　我已经对贵爵陈明了我的决心；
凭我们的神圣安息日我已发过誓，
必得要我应得的、照约的处罚；
如果您不准，就会有危难降落到
你们的宪章和城邦的自由风貌上。
您会问起我为什么宁愿有一磅
腐烂的臭肉，而不要三千金特格：
我不作答复：只是说，是我的性癖：
这是否回答了？假使我家里有只
耗子，我高兴花上一万金特格
把它毒死，怎么样？是否答复了？
有些人不爱瞧一只张口的猪仔；
有些人，瞧见一只猫会勃然大怒；
又有人，听到了风笛在哼哼鸣响，
会不禁流小便：因为爱憎和喜怒，
激情的主宰，指挥着它的意趣，

Of what it likes or loathes. Now, for your answer:
As there is no firm reason to be render'd,
Why he cannot abide a gaping pig;
Why he, a harmless necessary cat;
Why he, a wauling bagpipe; but of force
Must yield to such inevitable shame
As to offend, himself being offended;
So can I give no reason, nor I will not,
More than a lodg'd hate and a certain loathing
I bear Antonio, that I follow thus
A losing suit against him. Are you answered?

Bassanio This is no answer, thou unfeeling man,
To excuse the current of thy cruelty.

Shylock I am not bound to please thee with my answer.

Bassanio Do all men kill the things they do not love?

Shylock Hates any man the thing he would not kill?

Bassanio Every offence is not a hate at first.

Shylock What! wouldst thou have a serpent sting thee
    twice?

Antonio I pray you, think you question with the Jew:
You may as well go stand upon the beach,
And bid the main flood bate his usual height;
You may as well use question with the wolf,
Why he hath made the ewe bleat for the lamb;
You may as well forbid the mountain pines
To wag their high tops and to make no noise
When they are fretten with the gusts of heaven;
You may as well do anything most hard
As seek to soften that — than which what's harder? —
His Jewish heart: therefore, I do beseech you,
Make no moe offers, use no farther means,
But with all brief and plain conveniency.
Let me have judgment, and the Jew his will.

Bassanio For thy three thousand ducats here is six.

全凭一个人的好恶。关于您的答复：
没有什么稳固的理由可以举，
为何有人受不了张口的那只猪，
为何有人看不得无害的一只猫，
为何有人听不得套毛布的风笛声，
而要无可奈何地显出丑态来
惹恼人家，当他自己遭惹恼时；
故而我不能举理由，也不想揭举，
除了对安东尼奥我心中怀宿恨
和深固的憎恶，所以要对他进行
这无益的诉讼。我是否答复了您？

跋萨尼奥　这不是答复，你这无情的铁石人，
　　　　　它不能为你那残酷的行径辩解。
夏　洛　克　我所举的回答毋须讨你的欢喜。
跋萨尼奥　是否把不爱的东西都置之死地？
夏　洛　克　是否一个人，他恨的东西不愿杀？
跋萨尼奥　每一桩触犯开头并不是仇恨。
夏　洛　克　什么，你要一条蛇第二次咬你吗？
安东尼奥　我请你，要考虑跟这犹太人讲理：
　　　　　倒不如去到海滩上伫立着，
　　　　　叫大海的洪波减低它惯常的高度：
　　　　　你倒还不如去跟那贪狼问询，
　　　　　为何它使羊羔咩咩地叫母羊；
　　　　　你倒还不如去禁止山上的松林
　　　　　摇曳它们的高枝，不许发喧响，
　　　　　当它们被阵阵天风不断打扰时；
　　　　　你这是要作世上最艰难的事，
　　　　　来劝这犹太人变软他的心，——有什么
　　　　　比它更加硬？——故而，我恳切要求你，
　　　　　别再向他提商议，为我想方法，
　　　　　而要以完全爽快又简单的利便，
　　　　　让我受宣判，让犹太人逞他的意志。
跋萨尼奥　还你的三千特格，这里有六千。

Shylock　If every ducat in six thousand ducats
Were in six parts, and every part a ducat,
I would not draw them; I would have my bond.

Duke　How shalt thou hope for mercy, rendering none?

Shylock　What judgment shall I dread, doing no wrong?
You have among you many a purchas'd slave,
Which, fike your asses and your dogs and mules,
You use in abject and in slavish parts,
Because you bought them; shall I say to you
'Let them be free, marry them to your heirs?
Why sweat they under burdens? let their beds
Be made as soft as yours, and let their palates
Be season'd with such viands? You will answer
The slaves are ours. So do I answer you:
The pound of flesh which I demand of him
Is dearly bought; 'tis mine, and I will have it.
If you deny me, fie upon your law!
There is no force in the decrees of Venice.
I stand for judgment: answer; shall I have it?

Duke　Upon my power I may dismiss this court,
Unless Bellario, a learned doctor,
Whom I have sent for to determine this,
Come here to-day.

Salarino　　　　　My lord, here stays without
A messenger with letters from the doctor,
New come from Padua.

Duke　Bring us the letters; call the messenger.

Bassanio　Good cheer, Antonio! What, man, courage
　　yet!
The Jew shall have my flesh, blood, bones, and all,
Ere thou shalt lose for me one drop of blood.

Antonio　I am a tainted wether of the flock,
Meetest for death; the weakest kind of fruit

夏　洛　克　假使你那六千特格的每一块
　　　　　　都分成六份,每一份都是个特格,
　　　　　　我也不能接受;我只要执行立约。

公　　　爵　你这样寡情,怎么能希望得仁慈?

夏　洛　克　我没有做错事,有什么裁判可怕?
　　　　　　在你们中间有不少买来的奴隶,
　　　　　　他们跟你们的狗马驴骡一样,
　　　　　　你们待遇得好不鄙贱而卑微,
　　　　　　因为是你们购置的:我是否说道,
　　　　　　让他们自由,跟你们的子女婚配?
　　　　　　为什么他们在重负下流汗? 让他们
　　　　　　睡在同你们一般软的床上,吃喝
　　　　　　同样美味的食品? 你们会回答,
　　　　　　"这些奴隶是我们的";我同样回答你:
　　　　　　我向他要的这磅肉是出了高价
　　　　　　买来的;这是我的,我一定得有它。
　　　　　　你们若不给,你们的法律就完蛋!
　　　　　　威尼斯的法令被宣告没有效力。
　　　　　　我要求判决:回答我;给我,不给?

公　　　爵　凭我的权力,我可以停审缓判,
　　　　　　除非有培拉里奥,一位法学界
　　　　　　宏儒,我曾延请他到此来定案,
　　　　　　今天能出席。

萨勒里奥　　　　　　　　　　报贵爵,庭外有一名
　　　　　　使者来自帕度亚,送博士的信件。

公　　　爵　把信件交上来;叫使者来到庭上。

跋萨尼奥　且安心爽快吧,安东尼奥! 什么,
　　　　　　老兄鼓起勇气来! 这个犹太人
　　　　　　须得有我的血肉、骨骼和一切,
　　　　　　在你要为我流一滴血之前。

安东尼奥　我是羊群里一头有病毒的羯羊,
　　　　　　最该去死亡;最孱弱的果子最早

Drops earliest to the ground, and so let me.

You cannot better be employ'd, Bassanio,

Than to live still, and write mine epitaph.

[*Enter* Nerissa *dressed like a lawyer's clerk.*]

Duke   Came you from Padua, from Bellario?

Nerissa   From both, my lord. Bellario greets your Grace.

[*Presents a letter.*]

Bassanio   Why dost thou whet thy knife so earnestly?

Shylock   To cut the forfeiture from that bankrupt there.

Gratiano   Not on thy sole, but on thy soul, harsh Jew,

Thou mak'st thy knife keen; but no metal can,

No, not the hangman's axe, bear half the keenness

Of thy sharp envy. Can no prayers pierce thee?

Shylock   No, none that thou hast wit enough to make.

Gratiano   O, be thou damn'd, inexecrable dog!

And for thy life let justice be accus'd.

Thou almost mak'st me waver in my faith,

To hold opinion with Pythagoras

That souls of animals infuse themselves

Into the trunks of men. Thy currish spirit

Govern'd a wolf who, hang'd for human slaughter,

Even from the gallows did his fell soul fleet,

And, whilst thou lay'st in thy unhallow'd dam,

Infus'd itself in thee; for thy desires

Are wolfish, bloody, starv'd and ravenous.

Shylock   Till thou canst rail the seal from off my bond,

Thou but offend'st thy lungs to speak so loud;

Repair thy wit, good youth, or it will fall

To cureless ruin. I stand here for law.

Duke   This letter from Bellario doth commend

A young and learned doctor to our court.

坠落到地上;故而让我也这样:
你不能做更好的事,跋萨尼奥,
除了还活着,去写我的墓志铭。
　　　　　　　　［纳丽莎饰一律师的书记上。

公　　爵	你从帕度亚来吗,从培拉里奥处?
纳 丽 莎	正是的,贵爵。培拉里奥向阁下
	致问候。　　　　　　　［呈一信件。
跋 萨 尼 奥	为什么把刀子磨得这么急?
夏 洛 克	要割那破产的家伙身上一磅肉。
葛拉希阿诺	不是在你鞋底上,残酷的犹太人,

葛拉希阿诺　不是在你鞋底上,残酷的犹太人,
而是在你灵魂上,你磨砺你的刀;
可是再没有镔铁或精钢,没有,
即使是刽子手的行刑斧头也没有
你那锋利的恶毒一半那样
凶残又酷烈。什么祈求也穿不透?
夏 洛 克　不行,不论你说得多巧妙也不成。
葛拉希阿诺　啊,你这只准打入地狱、没法去
诅咒的恶狗! 你能活在这世上,
得叫公道被控告。你几乎使我
动摇了信仰,跟毕撒哥拉斯一起,
认为畜生的灵魂注入了人躯干;
你那恶毒的幽灵原管着一条狼,
那凶狼因杀人被绞死,绑在绞架上,
凶魂逃失时正值你躺在你那
肮脏的母体里,它就注入你身躯;
因你的欲望正像狼,极凶残、贪婪。
夏 洛 克　除非你能把借据上的印章骂掉,
你这样叫嚷只能把你的肺来伤:
保养你的心智,好少年,否则它会要
损毁破灭掉。我要求法律裁决。
公　　爵　培拉里奥这封信介绍了一位
年轻而博学的宏儒到我们庭上。

Where is he?

Nerissa He attendeth here hard by,

To know your answer, whether you'll admit him.

Duke of Venice With all my heart: some three or four of you

Go give him courteous conduct to this place.

Meantime, the court shall hear Bellario's letter.

Clerk [*Reads.*] *Your Grace shall understand that at the receipt of your letter I am very sick; but in the instant that your messenger came, in loving visitation was with me a young doctor of Rome; his name is Balthazar. I acquainted him with the cause in controversy between the Jew and Antonio the merchant; we turn'd o'er many books together; he is furnished with my opinion which, bettered with his own learning, — the greatness whereof I cannot enough commend, — comes with him at my importunity to fill up your Grace's request in my stead. I beseech you let his lack of years be no impediment to let him lack a reverend estimation, for I never knew so young a body with so old a head. I leave him to your gracious acceptance, whose trial shall better publish his commendation.*

Duke You hear the learn'd Bellario, what he writes;

And here, I take it, is the doctor come.

[*Enter* Portia, *dressed like a doctor of laws.*]

Give me your hand; come you from old Bellario?

Portia I did, my lord.

Duke You are welcome; take your place.

Are you acquainted with the difference

That holds this present question in the court?

Portia I am informed throughly of the cause.

Which is the merchant here, and which the Jew?

Duke of Venice Antonio and old Shylock, both stand forth.

Portia Is your name Shylock?

Shylock Shylock is my name.

Portia Of a strange nature is the suit you follow;

Yet in such rule that the Venetian law

他在哪里?

纳 丽 莎 　　　　　　他就在外边等候着,
听您的回音,是否让他上庭来。

公 爵 我一心欢迎。你们出去三四人,
延请他到庭上来。同时,这庭上
且聆听培拉里奥的这封来信。

书 记 〔念〕"贵爵可以了解到,当接奉来书时,我病患很深:
但正值贵介到来时,罗马有一位年轻博士正宠临舍
下;他的高名是巴尔萨什。我告知了他那犹太人和
商人安东尼奥之间发生的案情:我们遍查了许多典
籍:他具有了我的见解;敝见再加上他自己的学问,
其博大宏深我无法充分赞赏,他携带着,经我的恳
请,来替我满足您阁下的要求。我至希他年事不高
不会成为他得不到崇敬尊重的故障;因为我从未见
到过这样少年老成之士。我推举他给阁下的亲仁雅
顾,他的才学智慧实非过誉之辞。"

公 爵 你们听到了博学的培拉里奥,
他写的是什么,而现在,博士来了。

　　　　　〔宝喜霞上,扮一法学博士。

请将手给我。您是从培拉里奥
老法曹那里来的吗?

宝 喜 霞 　　　　　　正是,阁下。

公 爵 欢迎您:请就位。您是否已知道庭上
关于现在这讼案的争执意见?

宝 喜 霞 我已经熟知这案子的一切情实。
这里谁是那商人,谁是那犹太人?

公 爵 安东尼奥和犹太人,站上来。

宝 喜 霞 你可是名叫夏洛克?

夏 洛 克 　　　　　　我叫夏洛克。

宝 喜 霞 你进行的诉讼性质显得奇怪;
可是按常规,威尼斯的法律不能

Cannot impugn you as you do proceed.

[*To* Antonio.] You stand within his danger, do you not?

Antonio   Ay, so he says.

Portia   Do you confess the bond?

Antonio   I do.

Portia   Then must the Jew be merciful.

Shylock   On what compulsion must I? Tell me that.

Portia   The quality of mercy is not strain'd;

It droppeth as the gentle rain from heaven

Upon the place beneath. It is twice blest:

It blesseth him that gives and him that takes.

'Tis mightiest in the mightiest; it becomes

The throned monarch better than his crown;

His sceptre shows the force of temporal power,

The attribute to awe and majesty,

Wherein doth sit the dread and fear of kings;

But mercy is above this sceptred sway,

It is enthroned in the hearts of kings,

It is an attribute to God himself;

And earthly power doth then show likest God's

When mercy seasons justice. Therefore, Jew,

Though justice be thy plea, consider this,

That in the course of justice none of us

Should see salvation; we do pray for mercy,

And that same prayer doth teach us all to render

The deeds of mercy. I have spoke thus much

To mitigate the justice of thy plea,

Which if thou follow, this strict court of Venice

Must needs give sentence 'gainst the merchant there.

Shylock   My deeds upon my head! I crave the law,

The penalty and forfeit of my bond.

　　　　　　对你提出异议,当你起诉时。

　　　　　　〔对安〕你的安全被他所危及,是不是?

安 东 尼 奥　哦,他是这样说。

宝 　喜 　霞　　　　　　　　你承认借约吗?

安 东 尼 奥　我承认。

宝 　喜 　霞　　　　　那么,犹太人一定得仁慈。

夏 　洛 　克　根据什么我要被强制? 告诉我。

宝 　喜 　霞　仁慈的性质不含有任何勉强,

　　　　　　它好比甘雨一般从昊天下降到

　　　　　　人间地上:它双双赐福于人们;

　　　　　　施与者既得福,受惠者同样承恩:

　　　　　　它是最有权力者的最高权能:

　　　　　　它比王冕更适合于在位的君王;

　　　　　　王仗显示出人间权位的威力,

　　　　　　起敬畏和威严的表征,其中寓有着

　　　　　　对于君王们的畏惧和惶恐;但仁慈

　　　　　　却超越这个执掌王仗的权势;

　　　　　　它在君王们的心房里头登极,

　　　　　　它乃是上帝自己的一个徽征;

　　　　　　而人间权力会显得像是神权,

　　　　　　当仁慈调和着公道。故而,犹太人,

　　　　　　虽然你兴讼的要求是公道,

　　　　　　请考虑这点,就是,按公道的常理,

　　　　　　我们没有人将能得拯救:我们

　　　　　　都祈求仁慈,而这一祈祷就教

　　　　　　我们大家都去做仁慈的善行。

　　　　　　我说了这么许多来缓和你这件

　　　　　　诉讼所要求的公道:可是你如果

　　　　　　只追求这个,威尼斯这严谨的法庭

　　　　　　一定得对被告那个商人宣判。

夏 　洛 　克　我的事我自己承当! 我要求执法,

　　　　　　照我这债券施行破约的处罚。

Portia Is he not able to discharge the money?

Bassanio Yes; here I tender it for him in the court;
Yea, twice the sum; if that will not suffice,
I will be bound to pay it ten times o'er
On forfeit of my hands, my head, my heart;
If this will not suffice, it must appear
That malice bears down truth. And, I beseech you,
Wrest once the law to your authority;
To do a great right do a little wrong,
And curb this cruel devil of his will.

Portia It must not be; there is no power in Venice
Can alter a decree established;
'Twill be recorded for a precedent,
And many an error by the same example
Will rush into the state. It cannot be.

Shylock A Daniel come to judgment! Yea, a Daniel!
O wise young judge, how I do honour thee!

Portia I pray you, let me look upon the bond.

Shylock Here 'tis, most reverend doctor; here it is.

Portia Shylock, there's thrice thy money offer'd thee.

Shylock An oath, an oath! I have an oath in heaven.
Shall I lay perjury upon my soul?
No, not for Venice.

Portia   Why, this bond is forfeit;
And lawfully by this the Jew may claim
A pound of flesh, to be by him cut off
Nearest the merchant's heart. Be merciful.
Take thrice thy money; bid me tear the bond.

Shylock When it is paid according to the tenour.
It doth appear you are a worthy judge;
You know the law; your exposition
Hath been most sound; I charge you by the law,

宝　喜　霞	他是否不能清偿欠你的款子？
跋萨尼奥	是啊，这里我替他在庭上归还；
	是啊，这数目的两倍；如果还不够，
	我负责付还此数的十倍，再失约，
	处罚将是我的手、我的头、我的心：
	如果这样还不够，那定必显得
	恶意压倒了真理。我对您恳求，
	将法律扭捩到您的权威之下：
	为了做一件大好事，做一点小错，
	控制这残酷的魔鬼，使他不得逞。
宝　喜　霞	决不能这样做；威尼斯城邦没人
	有权能改变一项既定的律令；
	这会变作个成了存案的先例，
	跟着许多错误就援引这例子
	将会涌进国事中：不能这样做。
夏　洛　克	一位但尼尔裁判了！啊，但尼尔！
	年轻明智的法官，我多么崇敬您！
宝　喜　霞	请您给我瞧一瞧这一张借约。
夏　洛　克	在这里，最尊敬的博士，就在这里。
宝　喜　霞	夏洛克，有你款子的三倍还你呢。
夏　洛　克	发过誓，发过誓，我曾对天发过誓：
	我难道叫我的灵魂毁誓而犯罪吗？
	不行，整个威尼斯都给我也不成。
宝　喜　霞	是呀，按借约是该处罚的；据此，
	犹太人可依法要求一磅肉，由他
	割自最靠近这商人的心脏所在处。
	放仁慈些吧：收下三倍的钱数；
	叫我撕掉借约吧。
夏　洛　克	须待根据
	借约的规定付清了之后。看来
	您是位严正的法官；您通晓法律，
	所作的解释也极为确当；我请您，

Whereof you are a well-deserving pillar,

Proceed to judgment. By my soul I swear

There is no power in the tongue of man

To alter me. I stay here on my bond.

Antonio   Most heartily I do beseech the court

To give the judgment.

Portia   Why then, thus it is:

You must prepare your bosom for his knife.

Shylock   O noble judge! O excellent young man!

Portia   For the intent and purpose of the law

Hath full relation to the penalty,

Which here appeareth due upon the bond.

Shylock   'Tis very true. O wise and upright judge,

How much more elder art thou than thy looks!

Portia   Therefore, lay bare your bosom.

Shylock   Ay, 'his breast':

So says the bond: — doth it not, noble judge? —

Nearest his heart: those are the very words.

Portia   It is so. Are there balance here to weigh

The flesh?

Shylock   I have them ready.

Portia   Have by some surgeon, Shylock, on your charge,

To stop his wounds, lest he do bleed to death.

Shylock   Is it so nominated in the bond?

Portia   It is not so express'd; but what of that?

'Twere good you do so much for charity.

Shylock   I cannot find it; 'tis not in the bond.

Portia   You, merchant, have you anything to say?

Antonio   But little: I am arm'd and well prepar'd.

> 您乃是应受尊崇的法界的栋梁，
> 依据法律的名义，请您就进行
> 宣判:我凭我的灵魂发誓，决没有
> 人的喉舌有力量改变我的决心:
> 我现在立等要执行立约。

安 东 尼 奥　　　　　　　　　　　我也
> 诚心请堂上宣判。

宝 喜 霞　　　　　　　　　那么,就这样:
> 你须得准备把胸膛迎接他的刀。

夏 洛 克　啊,高贵的法官,英杰的年轻人!

宝 喜 霞　因为法律的用意和目的完全
> 符合这处罚,且已在约上到期。

夏 洛 克　非常正确:聪明又正直的法官!
> 您比您的相貌更要老成多少!

宝 喜 霞　故而就袒露你的胸膛。

夏 洛 克　　　　　　　　　　是啊,
> 他的胸膛:约上这么说:是不是,
> 高贵的法官?"最靠近他心脏",正是
> 这几个字儿。

宝 喜 霞　　　　　　　　　是这样。备好了天平
> 秤秤肉吗?

夏 洛 克　　　　　　　　我备好在此。

宝 喜 霞　夏洛克,由你去请一位外科医生,
> 去堵住创口,免得他流血致死。

夏 洛 克　借约里这样讲到吗?

宝 喜 霞　　　　　　　　　　没这样表明:
> 但那有什么关系? 为慈悲你做
> 这么点,乃是件好事。

夏 洛 克　　　　　　　　　这我找不到;
> 合约里没有写。

宝 喜 霞　　　　　　　　商人,你有什么话?

安 东 尼 奥　不多:我已有准备,充分预备好。

Give me your hand, Bassanio: fare you well!
Grieve not that I am fallen to this for you,
For herein Fortune shows herself more kind
Than is her custom: it is still her use
To let the wretched man outlive his wealth,
To view with hollow eye and wrinkled brow
An age of poverty; from which lingering penance
Of such misery doth she cut me off.
Commend me to your honourable wife:
Tell her the process of Antonio's end;
Say how I lov'd you; speak me fair in death;
And, when the tale is told, bid her be judge
Whether Bassanio had not once a love.
Repent but you that you shall lose your friend,
And he repents not that he pays your debt;
For if the Jew do cut but deep enough,
I'll pay it instantly with all my heart.

Bassanio   Antonio, I am married to a wife
Which is as dear to me as life itself;
But life itself, my wife, and all the world,
Are not with me esteem'd above thy life;
I would lose all, ay, sacrifice them all
Here to this devil, to deliver you.

Portia   Your wife would give you little thanks for that,
If she were by to hear you make the offer.

Gratiano   I have a wife whom, I protest, I love;
I would she were in heaven, so she could
Entreat some power to change this currish Jew.

Nerissa   'Tis well you offer it behind her back;
The wish would make else an unquiet house.

Shylock   These be the Christian husbands! I have a
         daughter;
Would any of the stock of Barabbas

将手伸给我，跋萨尼奥：祝平安！
别为我因替你出力受累而伤心：
因为在这件事上命运显现得
比她素常时较温存：她经常惯于
使堕入悲惨的苦难人遭到穷迫，
以凹陷的双目、皱蹙的眉宇苦度
老年的穷困，从这样的惩罚，迁延
而愁苦，她将我一举割除得爽利。
为我向光荣的新婚嫂子致意：
告诉她安东尼奥临终时的经过；
诉说我怎样爱你，又怎样从容
就死；待事故讲完后，要她作评断
说跋萨尼奥曾否有个真心
好友。莫懊丧你将失去这好友，
他也不懊丧他为你还债而丧生；
因为假使犹太人切得足够深，
我将顷刻间用我的全心作清偿。

跋萨尼奥 安东尼奥，我娶了一位好妻子，
她对我来说同生命一样珍贵；
但生命本身，我的妻，这整个世界，
我珍惜他们，并不过于珍惜你：
我宁愿失去这一切，嗳，牺牲掉
他们给这个魔鬼，来将你拯救。

宝 喜 霞 您妻子不会为了这句话感谢您，
假使她在旁，听您表这个心愿。

葛拉希阿诺 我有个妻子，我发誓我是爱她的：
我宁愿她此刻在天上，可以祈求
上帝去改变这条恶狗犹太佬。

纳 丽 莎 幸亏您在她背后作这样的献辞，
否则这愿望会叫您的家不安宁。

夏 洛 克 这些个就是基督教徒的丈夫了。
我有个女儿；但愿巴拉巴的子孙

Had been her husband, rather than a Christian!

We trifle time; I pray thee, pursue sentence.

Portia A pound of that same merchant's flesh is thine.

The court awards it and the law doth give it.

Shylock Most rightful judge!

Portia And you must cut this flesh from off his breast.

The law allows it and the court awards it.

Shylock Most learned judge! A sentence! Come, prepare.

Portia Tarry a little; there is something else.

This bond doth give thee here no jot of blood;

The words expressly are *a pound of flesh* :

Take then thy bond, take thou thy pound of flesh;

But, in the cutting it, if thou dost shed

One drop of Christian blood, thy lands and goods

Are, by the laws of Venice, confiscate

Unto the state of Venice.

Gratiano O upright judge! Mark, Jew: O learned judge!

Shylock Is that the law?

Portia   Thyself shalt see the act;

For, as thou urgest justice, be assur'd

Thou shalt have justice, more than thou desir'st.

Gratiano O learned judge! Mark, Jew: alearned judge!

Shylock I take this offer then: pay the bond thrice,

And let the Christian go.

Bassanio   Here is the money.

Portia Soft!

The Jew shall have all justice; soft! no haste: —

He shall have nothing but the penalty.

Gratiano O Jew! an upright judge, a learned judge!

是她的丈夫,也不要个基督教徒。
我们在浪费时间;我请您,就宣判。

宝　喜　霞　那商人身上的一磅肉归你所有:
这庭上判给你,法律给与了你。

夏　洛　克　极公正的法官!

宝　喜　霞　而你须得在他胸膛上割这肉:
法律允许这么办,这庭上判给你。

夏　洛　克　极博学的法官!判决了!来,预备!

宝　喜　霞　等一下;还有一些别的事。这借约
在此绝没有给你一滴血;写明的
只是"一磅肉":那么,按照这借约,
取你的这一磅肉;但割时若流了
这基督教徒的一滴血,你的地皮
和财货,按威城法律,要充公作为
威尼斯城邦所有。

葛拉希阿诺　啊,正直的法官!你瞧,犹太人:
啊,博学的法官!

夏　洛　克　　　　　　　　　法律是那样吗?

宝　喜　霞　你自己可以去查明法令;因为,
既然你坚持公道,要保证使你
能得到公道,超过你所愿有的。

葛拉希阿诺　啊,博学的法官!你瞧,犹太人;
一位博学的法官!

夏　洛　克　　　　　　　　　那么,我愿意
接受这提供;付给借约的三倍,
让这个基督教徒去。

跋萨尼奥　　　　　　　　　钱在这里。

宝　喜　霞　待一下!
这个犹太人得有全部的公道;
待一下!别着急:什么也不得给他,
只除是罚给他所有的。

葛拉希阿诺　　　　　　　　啊,犹太人!
一位正直的法官,博学的法官!

Portia Therefore, prepare thee to cut off the flesh.

Shed thou no blood; nor cut thou less nor more,

But just a pound of flesh: if thou tak'st more,

Or less, than a just pound, be it but so much

As makes it light or heavy in the substance,

Or the division of the twentieth part

Of one poor scruple; nay, if the scale do turn

But in the estimation of a hair,

Thou diest, and all thy goods are confiscate.

Gratiano A second Daniel, a Daniel, Jew!

Now, infidel, I have you on the hip.

Portia Why doth the Jew pause? Take thy forfeiture.

Shylock Give me my principal, and let me go.

Bassanio I have it ready for thee; here it is.

Portia He hath refus'd it in the open court;

He shall have merely justice, and his bond.

Gratiano A Daniel still say I; a second Daniel!

I thank thee, Jew, for teaching me that word.

Shylock Shall I not have barely my principal?

Portia Thou shalt have nothing but the forfeiture

To be so taken at thy peril, Jew.

Shylock Why, then the devil give him good of it!

I'll stay no longer question.

Portia   Tarry, Jew.

The law hath yet another hold on you.

It is enacted in the laws of Venice,

If it be prov'd against an alien

That by direct or indirect attempts

宝　喜　霞　　故而，预备好去割肉。你不得流血，
　　　　　　　　也不得少割或多割恰好一磅肉：
　　　　　　　　要是你多割或少割恰好一整磅，
　　　　　　　　只要份量上轻一点或者重一点，
　　　　　　　　相差只小小一分的二十份之一，
　　　　　　　　唔，天平上只相差头发丝那样
　　　　　　　　一丁点，你就得死，你全部的财货
　　　　　　　　要充公。

葛拉希阿诺　　　　　　但尼尔再生，但尼尔，犹太人！
　　　　　　　　现在邪教徒，我可是把你压倒了。

宝　喜　霞　　为什么这个犹太人踌躇？把罚给
　　　　　　　　你的东西拿去吧。

夏　洛　克　　　　　　　　把我的本金
　　　　　　　　还给我，让我去吧。

跋萨尼奥　　　　　　　我已经把钱
　　　　　　　　为你预备好；这里就是。

宝　喜　霞　　　　　　　　　他在
　　　　　　　　公开法庭上已经拒绝了还的钱：
　　　　　　　　他只能有他的公道和他的借约。

葛拉希阿诺　一位但尼尔，我说，但尼尔再生了！
　　　　　　　　多谢你，犹太人，你教我会说这话。

夏　洛　克　　我光是拿回本金都不行不成？

宝　喜　霞　　除了罚给你的东西，什么也不能
　　　　　　　　给你有，而你为取得它便得冒险。

夏　洛　克　　那么，魔鬼给他去保有这款子吧！
　　　　　　　　我不再在此供审问。

宝　喜　霞　　　　　　　　且慢，犹太人；
　　　　　　　　法律对于你另外有一项规定。
　　　　　　　　根据威尼斯所制定的一条法令，
　　　　　　　　假使对于一个外邦人经证明，
　　　　　　　　他以直接的或者间接的企图，

He seek the life of any citizen,
The party 'gainst the which he doth contrive
Shall seize one half his goods; the other half
Comes to the privy coffer of the state;
And the offender's life lies in the mercy
Of the duke only, 'gainst all other voice.
In which predicament, I say, thou stand'st;
For it appears by manifest proceeding
That indirectly, and directly too,
Thou hast contrived against the very life
Of the defendant; and thou hast incurr'd
The danger formerly by me rehears'd.
Down, therefore, and beg mercy of the duke.

Gratiano   Beg that thou mayst have leave to hang thyself;
And yet, thy wealth being forfeit to the state,
Thou hast not left the value of a cord;
Therefore thou must be hang'd at the state's charge.

Duke   That thou shalt see the difference of our spirits,
I pardon thee thy life before thou ask it.
For half thy wealth, it is Antonio's;
The other half comes to the general state,
Which humbleness may drive unto a fine.

Portia   Ay, for the state; not for Antonio.

Shylock   Nay, take my life and all, pardon not that:
You take my house when you do take the prop
That doth sustain my house; you take my life
When you do take the means whereby I live.

Portia   What mercy can you render him, Antonio?

Gratiano   A halter gratis; nothing else, for God's sake!

Antonio   So please my lord the Duke and all the court
To quit the fine for one half of his goods;

要谋害任何个本邦公民的生命，
那个他企图谋害的一造能取得
他财产的一半；另一半没入公库；
犯罪者的生命则撇开其他意见，
取决于公爵的仁慈。在这困境里，
我说，你正好已陷入；因为情况是，
根据明显的进程，你直接间接
已经谋害了这个被告的生命；
你是招致了我上面所说的危难。
故而跪下来，求公爵对你开恩。

葛拉希阿诺 恳求你可以被准许吊死自己；
可是你如今财产已经充了公，
你简直没有钱来买一根吊索；
因而你须得花国家的钱来行绞。

公　　爵 为使你见到我们精神的不同，
我在你请求之前赦免你的死刑；
你财产的一半，归安东尼奥所有；
另一半没入公库，你若是肯虚怀
而谦逊，可改成罚款。

宝　喜　霞 　　　　　　　　哎，那一份
公家的，安东尼奥这一份可不能。

夏　洛　克 不用，把我的生命和一切全拿去：
不必宽恩：你们拿走了支撑
我房子的支柱，就拿走了我的房子；
你们夺去了我安家活命的因由，
就剥夺了我的生命。

宝　喜　霞 安东尼奥，你能对于他施什么
仁慈？

葛拉希阿诺 　　　　送给他一根绞索；千万
不能给别的。

安 东 尼 奥 　　　　　公爵阁下和堂上
如今宽免了把他一半的财产

I am content, so he will let me have
The other half in use, to render it
Upon his death unto the gentleman
That lately stole his daughter:
Two things provided more, that, for this favour,
He presently become a Christian;
The other, that he do record a gift,
Here in the court, of all he dies possess'd
Unto his son Lorenzo and his daughter.

Duke   He shall do this, or else I do recant
The pardon that I late pronounced here.

Portia   Art thou contented, Jew? What dost thou say?

Shylock   I am content.

Portia   Clerk, draw a deed of gift.

Shylock   I pray you, give me leave to go from hence;
I am not well; send the deed after me
And I will sign it.

Duke   Get thee gone, but do it.

Gratiano   In christening shalt thou have two god-fathers;
Had I been judge, thou shouldst have had ten more,
To bring thee to the gallows, not to the font.

　　　　　　　　　　　　　　　　[*Exit* Shylock.]

Duke   Sir, I entreat you home with me to dinner.

Portia   I humbly do desire your Grace of pardon;
I must away this night toward Padua,
And it is meet I presently set forth.

Duke   I am sorry that your leisure serves you not.
Antonio, gratify this gentleman,
For in my mind you are much bound to him.

　　　　　　　　[*Exeunt* Duke, Magnificoes, *and Train.*]

Bassanio   Most worthy gentleman, I and my friend
Have by your wisdom been this day acquitted
Of grievous penalties; in lieu whereof

充公,我觉得安心;他将让我把
其他一半来使用,待到他死后
我把这给那个最近同他女儿
出奔的士子:此外还有两件事,
就是为感谢这恩情,他立即成为个
基督教徒;还有,他在这庭上
立下愿,将他死后的一切遗产
遗赠给他的女儿和女婿洛良佐。

公　　爵　他必须这么办,否则我就要
　　　　　取消我刚刚在这里宣布的宽宥。

宝　喜　霞　你可满意吗,犹太人? 你怎么说?

夏　洛　克　我满意。

宝　喜　霞　　　　　书记,立一张赠产业的文据。

夏　洛　克　请你们允许我退庭;我身体不好:
　　　　　把文据送给我,我将在上面签字。

公　　爵　你可以退庭,可是得签字。

葛拉希阿诺　　　　　　　　你在
　　　　　受洗礼的时候,须得有两位教父:
　　　　　我若是法官,你还得多加上十位,
　　　　　不是为你受洗,是送你上绞架。

　　　　　　　　　　　　　　　　［夏洛克下。

公　　爵　阁下,我请您到我家里去便餐。

宝　喜　霞　我敬请阁下多多原谅:我今夜
　　　　　必须赶往帕度亚,而正该现在
　　　　　就出发。

公　　爵　　　　　我很可惜您时间不许可。
　　　　　安东尼奥,对这位君子表感谢,
　　　　　因为,据我想,你多亏有他救助。

　　　　　　　　　　　　　　　　［公爵率随从下。

跋萨尼奥　最可尊贵的君子,我和我的朋友,
　　　　　经你的明智,今天得以解脱了
　　　　　可悲的刑罚;为表示我们的感荷,

Three thousand ducats, due unto the Jew,
We freely cope your courteous pains withal.

Antonio And stand indebted, over and above,
In love and service to you evermore.

Portia He is well paid that is well satisfied;
And I, delivering you, am satisfied,
And therein do account myself well paid:
My mind was never yet more mercenary.
I pray you, know me when we meet again:
I wish you well, and so I take my leave.

Bassanio Dear sir, of force I must attempt you further;
Take some remembrance of us, as a tribute,
Not as fee. Grant me two things, I pray you,
Not to deny me, and to pardon me.

Portia You press me far, and therefore I will yield.

[*To* Antonio]

Give me your gloves, I'll wear them for your sake.

[*To* Bassanio]

And, for your love, I'll take this ring from you.
Do not draw back your hand; I'll take no more;
And you in love shall not deny me this.

Bassanio This ring, good sir? alas, it is a trifle;
I will not shame myself to give you this.

Portia I will have nothing else but only this;
And now, methinks, I have a mind to it.

Bassanio There's more depends on this than on the value.
The dearest ring in Venice will I give you,
And find it out by proclamation:
Only for this, I pray you, pardon me.

Portia I see, sir, you are liberal in offers;
You taught me first to beg, and now methinks
You teach me how a beggar should be answer'd.

Bassanio Good sir, this ring was given me by my wife;
And, when she put it on, she made me vow

　　　　　　　这三千特格,原本负欠于犹太人,
　　　　　　　我们敬奉给阁下,报谢您的辛劳。

安东尼奥　我们还负欠深深,远不止此数,
　　　　　　　感恩而戴德,绵绵永没有终期。

宝　喜　霞　能得到衷心满意是最好的酬佣;
　　　　　　　而我,解救了你们,就感觉满意,
　　　　　　　在这件事上已得到充分的报偿:
　　　　　　　我的心智从没有谋利的意图。
　　　　　　　请两位以后再次见我时认识我:
　　　　　　　祝你们安康,我即此向两位告别。

跋萨尼奥　亲爱的阁下,我定得再对您请求:
　　　　　　　向我们取一点纪念品,作为敬礼,
　　　　　　　不作为酬谢:务请答应我两件事,
　　　　　　　不要拒绝我,要对我曲加原谅。

宝　喜　霞　你们情意太殷勤,我只好从命。
　　　　　　　[对安]将手套给我,我将戴它们纪念你;
　　　　　　　[对跋]为了你的爱,我要取这枚指环:
　　　　　　　别把手缩回去;我不要什么别的了;
　　　　　　　你一片情意,当也不会拒绝我。

跋萨尼奥　这指环,好台驾,啊也,它太不值钱!
　　　　　　　我不屑把它来奉赠给您阁下。

宝　喜　霞　我什么也不想要,只是要这个;
　　　　　　　现在我想我倒是很着意能有它。

跋萨尼奥　这指环本身,倒不在它值价多少。
　　　　　　　威尼斯最贵重的指环我要给您,
　　　　　　　我要出招告遍访这城邦去探寻:
　　　　　　　只是这一枚,我请您,要对我原谅。

宝　喜　霞　我见到,阁下,您提出给与很慷慨;
　　　　　　　您先是教我来乞讨;现在则我想
　　　　　　　您教我,一个乞丐该怎样去回绝。

跋萨尼奥　仁君,这指环是我妻子给我的;
　　　　　　　她戴上我这手指时,她要我发誓,

That I should neither sell, nor give, nor lose it.

Portia　That 'scuse serves many men to save their gifts.

And if your wife be not a mad-woman,

And know how well I have deserv'd this ring,

She would not hold out enemy for ever

For giving it to me. Well, peace be with you!

[Exeunt Portia *and* Nerissa. *]*

Antonio　My Lord Bassanio, let him have the ring:

Let his deservings, and my love withal,

Be valued 'gainst your wife's commandment.

Bassanio　Go, Gratiano, run and overtake him;

Give him the ring, and bring him, if thou canst,

Unto Antonio's house. Away! make haste.

[Exit Gratiano. *]*

Come, you and I will thither presently;

And in the morning early will we both

Fly toward Belmont. Come, Antonio.

[Exeunt.]

SCENE II. The same. *A street*

[Enter Portia *and* Nerissa. *]*

Portia　Inquire the Jew's house out, give him this deed,

And let him sign it; we'll away tonight,

And be a day before our husbands home.

This deed will be well welcome to Lorenzo.

[Enter Gratiano. *]*

Gratiano　Fair sir, you are well o'erta'en.

My Lord Bassanio, upon more advice,

Hath sent you here this ring, and doth entreat

Your company at dinner.

Portia　　　　　　　　That cannot be:

我决不将它卖掉、给掉或失掉。

宝　喜　霞　　那推托好给许多人来吝惜赠礼。
假使您妻子不是个发疯的女子，
且知道我多么该当有这枚指环，
她不会永远对您心存着敌意，
因为您给了我。好吧，祝你们平安。

〔宝喜霞与纳丽莎下。

安 东 尼 奥　　跋萨尼奥贵公子，请给他这指环：
望顾念他的大功，加上我的爱，
违犯一次新大嫂的阃闱命令吧。

跋 萨 尼 奥　　葛拉希阿诺，你去，将他追赶上；
给他这指环，且你若能够，请他到
安东尼奥家里来：去啊，要赶快。

〔葛下。

去来，你同我一起到你家里去；
明晨一清早我们飞往贝尔蒙：
来吧，安东尼奥。　　　　〔同下。

第 二 景

〔同前。一街道〕
〔宝喜霞与纳丽莎上。

宝　喜　霞　　打听出犹太人的家，给他这文据，
要他画上押：我们今夜就赶路，
能够比我们的丈夫早一天到家：
这文据洛良佐看到，准是很高兴。

〔葛拉希阿诺上。

葛拉希阿诺　　俊美的学士，我正好将您追赶上：
我们的跋萨尼奥贵公子考虑后，
将这枚指环奉送给阁下，还邀请
光临作餐叙。

宝　喜　霞　　　　　　　　餐叙恕不能奉陪：

His ring I do accept most thankfully;
And so, I pray you, tell him; furthermore,
I pray you show my youth old Shylock's house.

Gratiano　That will I do.

Nerissa　　　　　　　　Sir, I would speak with you.

　　　　　　　　　　　　　　　　[*Aside to* Portia.]

I'll see if I can get my husband's ring,
Which I did make him swear to keep for ever.

Portia　[*Aside To* Nerissa.]

Thou Mayst, I warrant. We shall have old swearing
That they did give the rings away to men;
But we'll outface them, and outswear them too.

[*Aloud*] Away! make haste; thou know'st where I will
　　tarry.

Nerissa　Come, good sir, will you show me to this house?

　　　　　　　　　　　　　　　　　[*Exeunt.*]

他这枚指环，我衷心感谢收下了：
请您就这样回报他：还有一件事，
请您指给我这小弟，夏洛克的家。

葛拉希阿诺 这由我来办。

纳 丽 莎 　　　　　　主座，我有话跟您说。
[对宝作旁白]我来试试把丈夫的指环弄到手，
我曾使他起过誓，永远不丢离。

宝 喜 霞 [对纳作旁白]我信你能够，我们将听到赌咒
发誓，他们所送给指环的是男子，
但我们将胜过他们，比他们赌得凶。
[高声]去吧，赶快：你晓得我将在哪里。

纳 丽 莎 来吧，士子，可能指给我他的家？　　　　　[同下。

ACT V.

SCENE I. Belmont. The *avenue* to Portia's *house*.

[*Enter* Lorenzo *and* Jessica.]

Lorenzo   The moon shines bright: in such a night as this,
When the sweet wind did gently kiss the trees,
And they did make no noise, in such a night,
Troilus methinks mounted the Troyan walls,
And sigh'd his soul toward the Grecian tents,
Where Cressid lay that night.

Jessica   In such a night
Did Thisby fearfully o'ertrip the dew,
And saw the lion's shadow ere himself,
And ran dismay'd away.

Lorenzo   In such a night
Stood Dido with a willow in her hand
Upon the wild sea-banks, and waft her love
To come again to Carthage.

Jessica   In such a night
Medea gather'd the enchanted herbs
That did renew old AEson.

Lorenzo   In such a night
Did Jessica steal from the wealthy Jew,

第 五 幕

第 一 景

[贝尔蒙。通至宝喜霞邸宅的林荫路]
[洛良佐与絮雪格上。

洛 良 佐　月色好光明:在这样一个夜晚,
　　　　　当和风轻轻地吻着丛丛的树木,
　　　　　它们默然无声息,在这样的夜晚,
　　　　　特洛壹勒斯登上特洛亚城墙,
　　　　　面对希腊军的营幕,想念寄身在
　　　　　那里的克瑞西,发出他心魂的悲叹。

絮 雪 格　在这样一个夜晚,昔斯俾惊心地
　　　　　踩着露水赴幽会,不见情人见一只
　　　　　狮子的影子而慌忙逃避。

洛 良 佐　　　　　　　　　　在这样
　　　　　一个夜晚,妲陀手持着柳枝,
　　　　　站在荒凉的海滩上,招她的情人
　　　　　回来到迦太基。

絮 雪 格　　　　　　　　在这样一个夜晚,
　　　　　美狄亚采集了神灵的仙草,使伊宋
　　　　　从衰朽回复到年少。

洛 良 佐　　　　　　　　　在这样一个
　　　　　夜晚,絮雪格从犹太富翁家出奔,

And with an unthrift love did run from Venice
As far as Belmont.

Jessica   In such a night
Did young Lorenzo swear he lov'd her well,
Stealing her soul with many vows of faith, —
And ne'er a true one.

Lorenzo   In such a night
Did pretty Jessica, like a little shrew,
Slander her love, and he forgave it her.

Jessica   I would out-night you, did no body come;
But, hark, I hear the footing of a man.

[*Enter* Stephano.]

Lorenzo   Who comes so fast in silence of the night?

Stephano   A friend.

Lorenzo   A friend! What friend? Your name, I pray you,
    friend?

Stephano   Stephano is my name, and I bring word
My mistress will before the break of day
Be here at Belmont; she doth stray about
By holy crosses, where she kneels and prays
For happy wedlock hours.

Lorenzo   Who comes with her?

Stephano   None but a holy hermit and her maid.
I pray you, is my master yet return'd?

Lorenzo   He is not, nor we have not heard from him.
But go we in, I pray thee, Jessica,
And ceremoniously let us prepare
Some welcome for the mistress of the house.

[*Enter* Launcelot.]

Launcelot. Sola, sola! wo ha, ho! sola, sola!

Lorenzo   Who calls?

Launcelot   Sola! Did you see Master Lorenzo?

跟一个不成材的情郎,打从威尼斯
直逃到贝尔蒙。

絮　雪　格　　　　　　　　在这样一个夜晚,
年轻的洛良佐发誓说是很爱她,
赌了好许多咒誓,偷了她的灵魂,
可没有一个是真的。

洛　良　佐　　　　　　　　　在这样一个
夜晚,美丽的絮雪格像个小泼妇,
诽谤她的情郎,他却原谅了她。

絮　雪　格　要是没人来,我能赛过你,唱彻
这夜宵;可是,你听,有人的脚步声。

　　　　　　　　　　[斯丹法诺上。

洛　良　佐　谁在这个静夜里来得这么快?

斯丹法诺　一个朋友。

洛　良　佐　一个朋友! 是什么朋友? 请问你,
朋友,你名叫什么?

斯丹法诺　　　　　　　　叫斯丹法诺;
我来报个信,我家女主人天明前
将来到贝尔蒙;她在圣迹灵碑间
盘桓了一两天,祈求祝祷她新婚
燕尔多幸福。

洛　良　佐　　　　　　　谁和她一同回家来?

斯丹法诺　没别人,只有修道士和她的伴娘。
请问您,主人家已经回来了没有?

洛　良　佐　他还没有呢,我们还没他的消息。
可是,我们里边去,请你,絮雪格,
让我们安排一些礼仪,预备
欢迎这邸宅的女主人。

　　　　　　　　　　[朗斯洛忒上。

朗斯洛忒　索拉,索拉! 喔哈,霍! 索拉,索拉!

洛　良　佐　谁在那儿嚷?

朗斯洛忒　索拉! 您见到洛良佐郎君不成?

Master Lorenzo! Sola, sola!

Lorenzo Leave holloaing, man. Here!

Launcelot Sola! Where? where?

Lorenzo Here!

Launcelot Tell him there's a post come from my master
with his horn full of good news; my master will be
here ere morning.

[*Exit.*]

Lorenzo Sweet soul, let's in, and there expect their
coming.

And yet no matter; why should we go in?

My friend Stephano, signify, I pray you,

Within the house, your mistress is at hand;

And bring your music forth into the air.

[*Exit* Stephano.]

How sweet the moonlight sleeps upon this bank!

Here will we sit and let the sounds of music

Creep in our ears; soft stillness and the night

Become the touches of sweet harmony.

Sit, Jessica: look how the floor of heaven

Is thick inlaid with patines of bright gold;

There's not the smallest orb which thou behold'st

But in his motion like an angel sings,

Still quiring to the young-eyed cherubins;

Such harmony is in immortal souls;

But, whilst this muddy vesture of decay

Doth grossly close it in, we cannot hear it.

[*Enter* Musicians.]

Come, ho! and wake Diana with a hymn;

With sweetest touches pierce your mistress' ear,

And draw her home with music.   [*Music.*]

Jessica I am never merry when I hear sweet music.

Lorenzo The reason is, your spirits are attentive;

For do but note a wild and wanton herd,

Or race of youthful and unhandled colts,

　　　　　洛良佐郎君,索拉,索拉!
洛　良　佐　别那么嚷嚷,人儿:在这里。
朗 斯 洛 忒　索拉! 哪里? 哪里?
洛　良　佐　这里。
朗 斯 洛 忒　告诉他,我家主人派个人儿带了一兜子好消息来啦:
　　　　　我家主人天明前要到这儿的。　　　　　　　　〔下。
洛　良　佐　好心肝,我们进去,等他们回来吧。
　　　　　可是没关系:为什么我们要进去?
　　　　　我这位朋友斯丹法诺,请你到
　　　　　里边去声言,你们的女主人就到来;
　　　　　你们带着乐器到外边来迎接。

　　　　　　　　　　　　　　　　〔斯丹法诺下。

　　　　　多甜啊,月光躺在这坡上在睡眠!
　　　　　我们就在此坐下,让音乐的声音
　　　　　沁入我们的耳朵:柔和的寂静
　　　　　与良宵,跟乐声的和谐调融为一。
　　　　　坐下,絜雪格。你瞧,这浅碧的天宇
　　　　　嵌满了灿烂的闪闪金光小碟儿,
　　　　　你所见到的每一颗最小的天球,
　　　　　无不在它转动中天使般唱着歌,
　　　　　永远应和着幼眼的天童们的歌唱;
　　　　　永生的灵魂都含有这样的和谐;
　　　　　但当这些个泥污的腐朽臭皮囊
　　　　　在外面包藏着,我们便无法听见。
　　　　　　　　〔乐人们上。
　　　　　来啊,奏一支圣歌来唤醒黛阿娜:
　　　　　用最最甜美的吹弹沁入你们
　　　　　女主人的耳朵,用乐声吸引她回家。
絜　雪　格　我听到柔和的乐声总心怀惆怅。
洛　良　佐　这是因为你的心灵异常敏感:
　　　　　只须看一群粗野天成的牛犊,
　　　　　或一簇未加驾驭过的青壮小马,

Fetching mad bounds, bellowing and neighing loud,
Which is the hot condition of their blood;
If they but hear perchance a trumpet sound,
Or any air of music touch their ears,
You shall perceive them make a mutual stand,
Their savage eyes turn'd to a modest gaze
By the sweet power of music: therefore the poet
Did feign that Orpheus drew trees, stones, and floods;
Since nought so stockish, hard, and full of rage,
But music for the time doth change his nature.
The man that hath no music in himself,
Nor is not mov'd with concord of sweet sounds,
Is fit for treasons, stratagems, and spoils;
The motions of his spirit are dull as night,
And his affections dark as Erebus.
Let no such man be trusted. Mark the music.

      [*Enter* Portia *and* Nerissa, *at a distance.*]

Portia   That light we see is burning in my hall.
How far that little candle throws his beams!
So shines a good deed in a naughty world.

Nerissa   When the moon shone, we did not see the candle.

Portia   So doth the greater glory dim the less:
A substitute shines brightly as a king
Until a king be by, and then his state
Empties itself, as doth an inland brook
Into the main of waters. Music! hark!

Nerissa   It is your music, madam, of the house.

Portia   Nothing is good, I see, without respect:
Methinks it sounds much sweeter than by day.

Nerissa   Silence bestows that virtue on it, madam.

奔腾跳跃着,不停地哞叫和鸣嘶,
原来那就是它们狂放的血性;
它们若偶尔听到了一声喇叭响,
或者有一曲乐声进它们的耳朵,
你就会见到它们都一齐立定,
它们犷野的眼光被柔和的乐声
所中,会变成温存的注视:故而
诗人编造出奥菲斯能移动木石、
奔注流水的故事;因为再没有
东西太蠢笨、死硬或生性猖狂,
音乐总能一时间改变它的性情。
所以那个人,他性灵之中没音乐,
也不能用美妙乐声的谐和感动他,
是会策划叛逆、奸谋和掠劫的;
这样的家伙的心灵黝暗如黑夜,
他的感情黑沉沉跟冥府一般:
这样的人儿不能信赖他。听乐声。

　　　　　[宝喜霞与纳丽莎遥上。

宝　喜　霞　我们瞧见的那光芒来自我客厅里。
　　　　　一支小小的蜡烛,光线多么远!
　　　　　在恶劣的世上做一桩好事便这样。

纳　丽　莎　月亮照耀时,我们便不见烛光。

宝　喜　霞　宏大的光辉使渺小的光芒晦隐。
　　　　　一个替代人照耀得显焕像君王,
　　　　　等到一位君主亲出场,那时节
　　　　　他的威严便消失,像一条溪流
　　　　　注入浩瀚的海洋。听啊! 这乐声!

纳　丽　莎　这是您府邸里的乐声,姑娘。

宝　喜　霞　　　　　　　　　　　　　没有
　　　　　东西是好的,我想,如果没比较;
　　　　　我觉得这要比在白云听到更幽妙。

纳　丽　莎　夜静使它显见得更美妙,姑娘。

Portia   The crow doth sing as sweetly as the lark
When neither is attended; and I think
The nightingale, if she should sing by day,
When every goose is cackling, would be thought
No better a musician than the wren.
How many things by season season'd are
To their right praise and true perfection!
Peace, ho! The moon sleeps with Endymion,
And would not be awak'd!

                                        [Music ceases.]

Lorenzo   That is the voice,
Or I am much deceiv'd, of Portia.

Portia   He knows me as the blind man knows the cuckoo,
By the bad voice.

Lorenzo   Dear lady, welcome home.

Portia   We have been praying for our husbands' welfare,
Which speed, we hope, the better for our words.
Are they return'd?

Lorenzo   Madam, they are not yet;
But there is come a messenger before,
To signify their coming.

Portia   Go in, Nerissa;
Give order to my servants that they take
No note at all of our being absent hence;
Nor you, Lorenzo; Jessica, nor you.

                                        [A tucket sounds.]

Lorenzo   Your husband is at hand; I hear his trumpet.
We are no tell-tales, madam, fear you not.

Portia   This night methinks is but the daylight sick;
It looks a little paler; 'tis a day
Such as the day is when the sun is hid.

                [Enter Bassanio, Antonio,
              Gratiano, and their Followers.]

宝　喜　霞　若是没有人欣赏,乌鸦会唱得
　　　　　　跟云雀一般美好,而且我想来,
　　　　　　那夜莺,假使它在白日里嘤鸣,
　　　　　　当时每一只鹅儿聒聒在喧噪,
　　　　　　会被当作比鸥鷀不高明的歌鸟。
　　　　　　多少东西会被有利的时机
　　　　　　烘托得给赞赏至于尽善尽美!
　　　　　　嗨,悄悄的! 月儿和她的安迪敏
　　　　　　在酣睡,不容去惊醒。　　　　　　　［乐声止。］

洛　良　佐　　　　　　　　　　　我若是没听错,
　　　　　　那是宝喜霞的声音。

宝　喜　霞　　　　　　　　　　我声音难听,
　　　　　　好像布谷鸟,一下给瞎子听出来。

洛　良　佐　亲爱的夫人,欢迎您回家。

宝　喜　霞　　　　　　　　　　　　我们
　　　　　　是在为我们的丈夫祝福,愿他们
　　　　　　因我们的祈祷更加得福。他们
　　　　　　回家了没有?

洛　良　佐　　　　　　　　夫人,他们还没有;
　　　　　　可是有一名使从先来报他们
　　　　　　就要来。

宝　喜　霞　　　　　　　里边去,纳丽莎;关照下人们,
　　　　　　他们不知道我们出过门;您也不,
　　　　　　洛良佐;絜雪格,您也不。　　　　［喇叭齐鸣。］

洛　良　佐　　　　　　　　　　您的郎君
　　　　　　就到了;我听到号声已经响:我们
　　　　　　不是搬嘴人,夫人;您不用担心。

宝　喜　霞　我看来这夜晚只是天光害了病,
　　　　　　它显得苍白些:它是这样个白天,
　　　　　　当太阳被云层所盖,没有了阳光。

　　　　　　［跋萨尼奥、安东尼奥、葛拉希阿诺及随从人等上。

Bassanio We should hold day with the Antipodes,
If you would walk in absence of the sun.

Portia Let me give light, but let me not be light,
For a light wife doth make a heavy husband,
And never be Bassanio so for me;
But God sort all! You are welcome home, my lord.

Bassanio I thank you, madam; give welcome to my
    friend;
This is the man, this is Antonio,
To whom I am so infinitely bound.

Portia You should in all sense be much bound to him,
For, as I hear, he was much bound for you.

Antonio No more than I am well acquitted of.

Portia Sir, you are very welcome to our house.
It must appear in other ways than words,
Therefore I scant this breathing courtesy.

Gratiano [*To* Nerissa]
By yonder moon I swear you do me wrong;
In faith, I gave it to the judge's clerk.
Would he were gelt that had it, for my part,
Since you do take it, love, so much at heart.

Portia A quarrel, ho, already! What's the matter?

Gratiano About a hoop of gold, a paltry ring
That she did give me, whose posy was
For all the world like cutlers' poetry
Upon a knife, *Love me, and leave me not*.

Nerissa What talk you of the posy, or the value?
You swore to me, when I did give it you,
That you would wear it till your hour of death,
And that it should lie with you in your grave;
Though not for me, yet for your vehement oaths,

跛萨尼奥　　您若是在没有太阳的地方走路，
　　　　　　我们将跟地球那一边的人们
　　　　　　共享着白昼。

宝　喜　霞　　　　　　　　让我发放出光明
　　　　　　可不要像光线那样轻飘；因为
　　　　　　一个轻飘的妻子会叫她丈夫
　　　　　　心头沉重，而跛萨尼奥可切莫
　　　　　　为了我如此：但一切由上帝主宰！
　　　　　　欢迎您回家，夫君。

跛萨尼奥　　　　　　　　　　多谢您，细君。
　　　　　　欢迎我这位朋友。就是这个人，
　　　　　　我从这安东尼奥，真受惠无穷。

宝　喜　霞　　您当真是从他那里受惠无穷，
　　　　　　因为，我听说，为了您，他受累无穷。

安东尼奥　　算不了什么，现在一切都已经
　　　　　　解决了。

宝　喜　霞　　　　　大兄长，万分欢迎您光临：
　　　　　　这须得不是凭言语，要真心表示，
　　　　　　所以我一切客套的空话不说了。

葛拉希阿诺　〔对纳〕凭那边的月亮我起誓，您冤枉了我；
　　　　　　当真，我将它给了个法官的书记：
　　　　　　既然您，好人，把这事看得这么重，
　　　　　　我但愿要去的那人是个小太监。

宝　喜　霞　　啊哈，已经在吵架了！是为什么事？

葛拉希阿诺　为了个金圈儿，她给我的那只
　　　　　　不值钱的指环，上面刻着的铭文，
　　　　　　简直跟刀箭匠刻在刀上的诗句
　　　　　　一模一样，说什么"爱我，毋相弃"。

纳　丽　莎　您管它什么铭文，什么不值钱？
　　　　　　我当初给您的时分，您对我发誓，
　　　　　　说您将戴着它一直到您临死时，
　　　　　　说它将跟着您葬在您的坟墓里：
　　　　　　即令不为我，也要为您的重誓，

You should have been respective and have kept it.

Gave it a judge's clerk! No, God's my judge,

The clerk will ne'er wear hair on's face that had it.

Gratiano   He will, an if he live to be a man.

Nerissa   Ay, if a woman live to be a man.

Gratiano   Now, by this hand, I gave it to a youth,

A kind of boy, a little scrubbed boy

No higher than thyself, the judge's clerk;

A prating boy that begg'd it as a fee;

I could not for my heart deny it him.

Portia   You were to blame, — I must be plain with you, —

To part so slightly with your wife's first gift,

A thing stuck on with oaths upon your finger,

And so riveted with faith unto your flesh.

I gave my love a ring, and made him swear

Never to part with it, and here he stands,

I dare be sworn for him he would not leave it

Nor pluck it from his finger for the wealth

That the world masters. Now, in faith, Gratiano,

You give your wife too unkind a cause of grief;

An 'twere to me, I should be mad at it.

Bassanio   [*Aside.*]

Why, I were best to cut my left hand off,

And swear I lost the ring defending it.

Gratiano   My Lord Bassanio gave his ring away

Unto the judge that begg'd it, and indeed

Deserv'd it too; and then the boy, his clerk,

That took some pains in writing, he begg'd mine;

您该当把它重视而保存下来。
给了个法官的书记！不，上帝
是我的法官，那个拿指环的书记
脸上永远不会长上毛。

葛拉希阿诺　　　　　　　　　　他会的，
当他长大成人时。

纳　丽　莎　　　　　　　是啊，如果说
一个女人会变成个男子。

葛拉希阿诺　　　　　　　　　　凭我
这只手我打赌，我把它给了个少年，
像是个孩子，发育不全的小家伙，
并不比您高，是那法官的书记。
那是个多话的孩子，讨去作酬劳：
我实在拗不过，没有法子给了他。

宝　喜　霞　是您的不是，我须得跟您说分明，
这么轻易地把您妻子的第一件
礼物白送掉；那是用誓言裁在您
手指上，以诚信紧箍在您骨肉上。
我给了心上人一枚指环，要他
发誓永远不脱手；他现在在这里；
我敢为他发誓他决不会脱手，
或卸下他的手指头，即使是为了
全世界的财富。当真，葛拉希阿诺，
您给了您妻子太过伤心的因由：
若是我的话，我真要恼得不答应。

跋　萨　尼　奥　[旁白]嗳呀，我最好还是斩掉了这左手，
好发誓因保卫这指环才失掉了它。

葛拉希阿诺　跋萨尼奥公子送掉他的指环，
因为那法官向他讨，而他确实
应当有这个作报酬；跟着，那孩子，
他的书记，为谢他抄写上的辛苦，
讨了我的去；他们主仆两个人，

And neither man nor master would take aught
But the two rings.

Portia   What ring gave you, my lord?
Not that, I hope, which you receiv'd of me.

Bassanio   If I could add a lie unto a fault,
I would deny it; but you see my finger
Hath not the ring upon it; it is gone.

Portia   Even so void is your false heart of truth;
By heaven, I will ne'er come in your bed
Until I see the ring.

Nerissa   Nor I in yours
Till I again see mine.

Bassanio   Sweet Portia,
If you did know to whom I gave the ring,
If you did know for whom I gave the ring,
And would conceive for what I gave the ring,
And how unwillingly I left the ring,
When nought would be accepted but the ring,
You would abate the strength of your displeasure.

Portia   If you had known the virtue of the ring,
Or half her worthiness that gave the ring,
Or your own honour to contain the ring,
You would not then have parted with the ring.
What man is there so much unreasonable,
If you had pleas'd to have defended it
With any terms of zeal, wanted the modesty
To urge the thing held as a ceremony?
Nerissa teaches me what to believe:
I'll die for't but some woman had the ring.

Bassanio   No, by my honour, madam, by my soul,
No woman had it, but a civil doctor,
Which did refuse three thousand ducats of me,

什么也不要，只要这两枚指环。

宝　喜　霞　您送掉什么指环，夫君？我希望
　　　　　　不是那只我给的。

跋 萨 尼 奥　　　　　我若在错误上
　　　　　　再加撒谎，我便会否认：可是您
　　　　　　见到我手指上已没有指环：它是
　　　　　　没有了。

宝　喜　霞　　　　您的假真心是这么空虚。
　　　　　　我对天发誓，我决不会跟您同床，
　　　　　　要等见到了这指环。

纳　丽　莎　　　　　　我也不会上
　　　　　　您的床，要等见到了我的才算数。

跋 萨 尼 奥　亲爱的宝喜霞，
　　　　　　您若知道我给了什么人这指环，
　　　　　　您若知道我为谁给了这指环，
　　　　　　并且能设想为什么我给这指环，
　　　　　　以及我多么不愿给掉这指环，
　　　　　　当什么也不肯接受，只除这指环，
　　　　　　您是会减轻您这层不快之感的。

宝　喜　霞　您若知道这指环有什么好处，
　　　　　　或是给指环的那人的一半美德，
　　　　　　或是保存这指环您有何光荣，
　　　　　　您就不会轻易地捐弃这指环。
　　　　　　天下有什么人这样不讲道理，
　　　　　　假使您只要高兴用一点热情
　　　　　　保卫它，那人会那么缺乏礼让，
　　　　　　非拿去人家作礼仪的东西不可？
　　　　　　纳丽莎教了我相信是怎么回事：
　　　　　　我誓死认为是什么女人家拿了去。

跋 萨 尼 奥　不是，凭我的荣誉，凭我的灵魂，
　　　　　　细君，不是什么女人家，是一位
　　　　　　法学博士，他不受我三千金特格，

And begg'd the ring; the which I did deny him,

And suffer'd him to go displeas'd away;

Even he that had held up the very life

Of my dear friend. What should I say, sweet lady?

I was enforc'd to send it after him;

I was beset with shame and courtesy;

My honour would not let ingratitude

So much besmear it. Pardon me, good lady;

For, by these blessed candles of the night,

Had you been there, I think you would have begg'd

The ring of me to give the worthy doctor.

Portia Let not that doctor e'er come near my house;

Since he hath got the jewel that I loved,

And that which you did swear to keep for me,

I will become as liberal as you;

I'll not deny him anything I have,

No, not my body, nor my husband's bed.

Know him I shall, I am well sure of it.

Lie not a night from home; watch me like Argus;

If you do not, if I be left alone,

Now, by mine honour which is yet mine own,

I'll have that doctor for mine bedfellow.

Nerissa And I his clerk; therefore be well advis'd

How you do leave me to mine own protection.

Gratiano Well, do you so: let not me take him then;

For, if I do, I'll mar the young clerk's pen.

Antonio I am the unhappy subject of these quarrels.

Portia Sir, grieve not you; you are welcome notwithstanding.

Bassanio Portia, forgive me this enforced wrong;

却讨我这指环；我起初回绝了他，
让他不欢而别去；就是这个人，
他救了我这位亲爱的好友的生命。
我该说什么，好夫人？我被迫随后
送给他，我满腔的羞惭，情理不容我
不那样；我的荣誉不容许给忘恩
负义所污毁。宽恕了我吧，好夫人；
因为，凭这无数天上的圣烛光
我起誓，您当时如果在场，我相信
您也会央我将指环送给这博士。

宝 喜 霞　别让那博士来近我这宅邸：
既然他已到手了我爱的那珍宝，
那是您曾起过誓要替我保存的，
我便要变得和您同样地慷慨；
我不会对他吝惜我所有的一切，
不惜我自己的身体，我丈夫的床：
我定要认识他，这是肯定无疑的：
故而，一宵也不要宿歇在外边；
像个百眼怪那样守着我；您若是
不那样，留我成孤单一个人，那时节，
凭我的光荣，这还是我自己的所有，
我将叫那个博士跟我同衾枕。

纳 丽 莎　我要他的书记也这样；故而要当心，
您如果撇下我独白一人的辰光。

葛拉希阿诺　好吧，您便这么办；那么，别让我
抓到他；否则的话，我将折断
那少年书记的笔。

安 东 尼 奥　　　　　　　这场吵架
都是我起的因由。

宝 喜 霞　　　　　　　　大兄长，莫难受；
您是照样欢迎的。

跛 萨 尼 奥　　　　　　　宝喜霞，请恕我

And in the hearing of these many friends
I swear to thee, even by thine own fair eyes,
Wherein I see myself, —

Portia   Mark you but that!
In both my eyes he doubly sees himself,
In each eye one; swear by your double self,
And there's an oath of credit.

Bassanio   Nay, but hear me:
Pardon this fault, and by my soul I swear
I never more will break an oath with thee.

Antonio I once did lend my body for his wealth,
Which, but for him that had your husband's ring,
Had quite miscarried; I dare be bound again,
My soul upon the forfeit, that your lord
Will never more break faith advisedly.

Portia Then you shall be his surety. Give him this,
And bid him keep it better than the other.

Antonio Here, Lord Bassanio, swear to keep this ring.

Bassanio By heaven! it is the same I gave the doctor!

Portia I had it of him: pardon me, Bassanio,
For, by this ring, the doctor lay with me.

Nerissa And pardon me, my gentle Gratiano,
For that same scrubbed boy, the doctor's clerk,
In lieu of this, last night did lie with me.

Gratiano Why, this is like the mending of high ways

这个硬加在我头上的过错;而且
这么许多朋友都在此能听到,
我对您起誓,凭您的这双美目,
在其中我见到我自己——

宝　喜　霞　　　　　　　　　你们且听他!
在我两只眼睛里他双重瞧见
他自己;每一只眼睛里一个人;凭您
双重的人格去发誓,那便是您所谓
信用的誓言。

跋萨尼奥　　　　　　不然,可是听我说;
宽恕这过错,凭我的灵魂我发誓,
我将决不再违反我对您的誓言。

安东尼奥　我曾有一次借我的生命为他
筹财富;若不是由于有了您夫君
那只指环的那个人一力相挽救,
我这条性命早已完结了:我敢于
再作保,我的灵魂作抵押,您夫君
决不会再一次故意毁信破誓约。

宝　喜　霞　那么,要请您替他作担保。将这个
给他,叫他要保存得比那只更好。

安东尼奥　这儿,跋萨尼奥贵公子,宣誓
你要保全这指环。

跋萨尼奥　　　　　　天啊,这就是
我给那博士的!

宝　喜　霞　　　　　我从他那里得来的:
原谅我,跋萨尼奥;因为,凭这只
指环我起誓,那博士昨夜同我睡。

纳　丽　莎　对我也原谅,温蔼的葛拉希阿诺;
因为那个发育不全的小家伙,
那博士的书记,为了这指环昨夜
也跟我同眠宿。

葛拉希阿诺　　　　　嗳呀,这好像在夏天

In summer, where the ways are fair enough.

What! are we cuckolds ere we have deserv'd it?

Portia   Speak not so grossly. You are all amaz'd:

Here is a letter; read it at your leisure;

It comes from Padua, from Bellario:

There you shall find that Portia was the doctor,

Nerissa there, her clerk: Lorenzo here

Shall witness I set forth as soon as you,

And even but now return'd; I have not yet

Enter'd my house. Antonio, you are welcome;

And I have better news in store for you

Than you expect: unseal this letter soon;

There you shall find three of your argosies

Are richly come to harbour suddenly.

You shall not know by what strange accident

I chanced on this letter.

Antonio   I am dumb.

Bassanio   Were you the doctor, and I knew you not?

Gratiano   Were you the clerk that is to make me cuckold?

Nerissa   Ay, but the clerk that never means to do it,

Unless he live until he be a man.

Bassanio   Sweet doctor, you shall be my bedfellow:

When I am absent, then lie with my wife.

Antonio   Sweet lady, you have given me life and living;

For here I read for certain that my ships

Are safely come to road.

Portia   How now, Lorenzo!

My clerk hath some good comforts too for you.

Nerissa   Ay, and I'll give them him without a fee.

修公路,那时节路面铺得很平整:
什么,我们就平白当上了王八吗?

宝　喜　霞　　别说得这样粗俗。你们都诧异:
这里有封信;你们有空时念念它;
这是从帕度亚来的,自贝拉里奥:
从信里可知宝喜霞就是那博士,
纳丽莎是她的书记:洛良佐在此
将作证,我和你们是同时出发的,
只适才刚回来;我还没有进屋门。
安东尼奥,欢迎您光临;我还有
比您所预期的更好的消息保存着
给您:请您就打开这封信;在那里
您将发现您三艘满载的海舶
忽然进了港:您不会想到,因什么
难期的意外我会碰上这封信。

安 东 尼 奥　我惊奇得哑口无言了。

跋 萨 尼 奥　　　　　　　您就是
那博士而我认不出您吗?

葛拉希阿诺　　　　　　　　您就是
那书记而叫我当上王八吗?

纳　丽　莎　　　　　　　　　唔,
可是那书记决不想做那件事,
除非他长大成了人。

跋 萨 尼 奥　　　　　　　甜蜜的博士,
您得做我的同床人:当我不在时,
跟我的妻子共衾枕。

安 东 尼 奥　　　　　　　可爱的夫人,
您给了我生命和生活;因为在此
我得知,我的船舶已安全进了港。

宝　喜　霞　　怎么样,洛良佐? 我的书记也有些
安愉给与您。

纳　丽　莎　　　　　　　哦,我将把它们

There do I give to you and Jessica,
From the rich Jew, a special deed of gift,
After his death, of all he dies possess'd of.

Lorenzo   Fair ladies, you drop manna in the way
Of starved people.

Portia   It is almost morning,
And yet I am sure you are not satisfied
Of these events at full. Let us go in;
And charge us there upon inter'gatories,
And we will answer all things faithfully.

Gratiano   Let it be so: he first inter'gatory
That my Nerissa shall be sworn on is,
Whe'r till the next night she had rather stay,
Or go to bed now, being two hours to day:
But were the day come, I should wish it dark,
Till I were couching with the doctor's clerk.
Well, while I live, I'll fear no other thing
So sore as keeping safe Nerissa's ring.

[Exeunt.]

给与他，不收什么费。那里我给与
您和絜雪格，出自那犹太富翁，
一纸赠与的特别文据，说是
他死后，他给您他所有的一切遗产。

洛　良　佐　姣好的夫人们，你们在饥民面前
降落了甘露。

宝　喜　霞　　　　　　　天差点就要亮了。
可是我确信你们还要把事情
知道得更加详情些。我们里边去；
你们可以向我们详细询问，
我们会诚心把一切尽情回答。

葛拉希阿诺　就这样好了：第一个询问要求
我的纳丽莎宣誓申言的乃是，
她是否愿意等到第二天夜幕上，
还是现在离天明两小时就上床：
但若是白日来临，我愿它变昏沉，
我方好同那博士的书记同衾枕。
好吧，我活着什么东西都不怕，
只怕丢了纳丽莎的指环祸事大。

[同下。

图书在版编目(CIP)数据

威尼斯商人/〔英〕莎士比亚著;孙大雨译.
—上海:上海三联书店,2018.

ISBN 978 - 7 - 5426 - 6176 - 0

Ⅰ.①威… Ⅱ.①莎… ②孙… Ⅲ.①喜剧—剧本—
英国—中世纪 Ⅳ.①I561.33

中国版本图书馆 CIP 数据核字(2017)第 320741 号

威尼斯商人(中英文双语对照)

著　　者　〔英〕威廉·莎士比亚
译　　者　孙大雨

责任编辑　钱震华
装帧设计　陈益平

出版发行　上海三联书店
　　　　　(201199)中国上海市都市路 4855 号
印　　刷　上海昌鑫龙印务有限公司

版　　次　2018 年 4 月第 1 版
印　　次　2018 年 4 月第 1 次印刷
开　　本　890×1240　1/32
字　　数　180 千字
印　　张　6.25
书　　号　ISBN 978 - 7 - 5426 - 6176 - 0/I·1363
定　　价　30.00 元